Concerning Cats

Helen M. Winslow

Contents

CONCERNING CATS

BY

Helen M. Winslow

To the

"PRETTY LADY"

WHO NEVER BETRAYED A SECRET, BROKE A PROMISE, OR
PROVED AN UNFAITHFUL FRIEND; WHO HAD
ALL THE VIRTUES AND NONE OF
THE FAILINGS OF HER SEX

I Dedicate this Volume

CHAPTER I
CONCERNING THE "PRETTY LADY"

She was such a Pretty Lady, and gentle withal; so quiet and eminently lady-like in her behavior, and yet dignified and haughtily reserved as a duchess. Still it is better, under certain circumstances, to be a cat than to be a duchess. And no duchess of the realm ever had more faithful retainers or half so abject subjects.

Do not tell me that cats never love people; that only places have real hold upon their affections. The Pretty Lady was contented wherever I, her most humble slave, went with her. She migrated with me from boarding-house to sea-shore cottage; then to regular housekeeping; up to the mountains for a summer, and back home, a long day's journey on the railway; and her attitude was always "Wheresoever thou goest I will go, and thy people shall be my people."

I have known, and loved, and studied many cats, but my knowledge of her alone would convince me that cats love people--in their dignified, reserved way, and when they feel that their love is not wasted; that they reason, and that they seldom act from impulse.

I do not remember that I was born with an inordinate fondness for cats; or that I cried for them as an infant. I do not know, even, that my childhood was marked by an overweening pride in them; this, perhaps, was because my cruel parents established a decree, rigid and unbending as the laws of the Medes and Persians, that we must never have more than one cat at a time. Although this very law may argue that predilection, at an early age, for harboring everything feline which came in my way, which has since become at once a source of comfort and distraction.

After a succession of feline dynasties, the kings and queens of which were handsome, ugly, sleek, forlorn, black, white, deaf, spotted, and otherwise marked, I remember fastening my affections securely upon one kitten who grew up to be the ugliest, gauntest, and dingiest specimen I ever have seen. In the days of his kitten-hood I christened him "Tassie" after his mother; but as time sped on, and the name hardly comported with masculine dignity, this was changed to Tacitus, as more befitting his sex. He had a habit of dodging in and out of the front door, which was heavy, and which sometimes swung together before he was well out of it. As a consequence, a caudal appendage with two broken joints was one of his distinguishing features. Besides a broken tail, he had ears which bore the marks of many a hard-fought battle, and an expression which for general "lone and lorn"-ness would have discouraged even Mrs. Gummidge. But I loved him, and judging from the disconsolate and long-continued wailing with which he rilled the house whenever I was away, my affection was not unrequited.

But my real thraldom did not begin until I took the Pretty Lady's mother. We had not been a week in our first house before a handsomely striped tabby, with eyes like beautiful emeralds, who had been the pet and pride of the next-door neighbor for five years, came over and domiciled herself. In due course of time she proudly presented us with five kittens. Educated in the belief that one cat was all that was compatible with respectability, I had four immediately disposed of, keeping the prettiest one, which grew up into the beautiful, fascinating, and seductive maltese "Pretty Lady," with white trimmings to her coat. The mother of Pretty Lady used to catch two mice at a time, and bringing them in together, lay one at my feet and say as plainly as cat language can say, "There, you eat that one, and I'll eat this," and then seem much surprised and disgusted that I had not devoured mine when she had finished her meal.

We were occupying a furnished house for the summer, however, and as we were to board through the winter, I took only the kitten back to town, thinking the mother would return to her former home, just over the fence. But no. For two weeks she refused all food and would not once enter the other house. Then I went out for her, and hearing my voice she came in and sat down before me, literally scolding me for a quarter of an hour. I shall be laughed at, but actual tears stood in her lovely green eyes and ran down her aristocratic nose, attesting her grief and accusing me, louder than her wailing, of perfidy.

I could not keep her. She would not return to her old home. I finally compromised by carrying her in a covered basket a mile and a half and bestowing her upon a friend who loves cats nearly as well as I. But although she was petted, and praised, and fed on the choicest of delicacies, she would not be resigned. After six weeks of mourning, she disappeared, and never was heard of more. Whether she sought a new and more constant mistress, or whether, in her grief at my shameless abandonment of her, she went to some lonely pier and threw herself off the dock, will never be known. But her reproachful gaze and tearful emerald eyes haunted me all winter. Many a restless night did I have to reproach myself for abandoning a creature who so truly loved me; and in many a dream did she return to heap shame and ignominy upon my repentant head.

This experience determined me to cherish her daughter, whom, rather, I cherished as her son, until there were three little new-born kittens, which in a moment of ignorance I "disposed of" at once. Naturally, the young mother fell exceedingly ill. In the most pathetic way she dragged herself after me, moaning and beseeching for help. Finally, I succumbed, went to a neighbor's where several superfluous kittens had arrived the night before, and begged one. It was a little black fellow, cold and half dead; but the Pretty Lady was beside herself with joy when I bestowed it upon her. For two days she would not leave the box where I established their headquarters, and for months she refused to wean it, or to look upon it as less than absolutely perfect. I may say that the Pretty Lady lived to be nine years old, and had, during that brief period, no less than ninety-three kittens, besides two adopted ones; but never did she bestow upon any of her own offspring that wealth of pride and affection which was showered upon black Bobbie.

When the first child of her adoption was two weeks old, I was ill one morning, and did not appear at breakfast. It had always been her custom to wait for my coming down in the morning, evidently considering it a not unimportant part of her duty to see me well launched for the day. Usually she sat at the head of the stairs and waited patiently until she heard me moving about. Sometimes she came in and sat on a chair at the head of my bed, or gently touched my face with her nose or paw. Although she knew she was at liberty to sleep in my room, she seldom did so, except when she had an infant on her hands. At first she invariably kept him in a lower drawer of my bureau. When he was large enough, she removed him to the foot of the bed, where for a week or two her maternal solicitude and sociable habits of nocturnal conversation with her progeny interfered seriously with my night's rest. If my friends used to notice a wild and haggard appearance of unrest about me at certain periods of the year, the reason stands here confessed.

I was ill when black Bobbie was two weeks old. The Pretty Lady waited until breakfast was over, and as I did not appear, came up and jumped on the bed, where she manifested some curiosity as to my lack of active interest in the world's affairs.

"Now, pussy," I said, putting out my hand and stroking her back, "I'm sick this morning. When you were sick, I went and got you a kitten. Can't you get me one?"

This was all. My sister came in then and spoke to me, and the Pretty Lady left us at once; but in less than two minutes she came back with her cherished kitten in her mouth. Depositing him in my neck, she stood and looked at me, as much as to say:--

"There, you can take him awhile. He cured me and I won't be selfish; I will share him with you."

I was ill for three days, and all that time the kitten was kept with me. When his mother wanted him, she kept him on the foot of the bed, where she nursed, and lapped, and scrubbed him until it seemed as if she must wear even his stolid nerves completely out. But whenever she felt like going out she brought him up and tucked him away in the hollow of my neck, with a little guttural noise that, interpreted, meant:--

"There, now you take care of him awhile. I'm all tired out. Don't wake him up."

But when the infant had dropped soundly asleep, she invariably came back and demanded him; and not only demanded, but dragged him forth from his lair by the nape of the neck, shrieking and protesting, to the foot of the bed again, where he was obliged to go through another course of scrubbing and vigorous maternal attentions that actually kept his fur from growing as fast as the coats of less devotedly cared-for kittens grow.

When I was well enough to leave my room, she transferred him to my lower bureau drawer, and then to a vantage-point behind an old lounge. But she never doubted, apparently, that it was the loan of that kitten that rescued me from an untimely grave.

I have lost many an hour of much-needed sleep from my cat's habit of coming upstairs at four A.M. and jumping suddenly upon the bed; perhaps landing on the pit of my stomach. Waking in that fashion, unsympathetic persons would have pardoned me if I had indulged in injudicious language, or had even thrown the cat violently from my otherwise peaceful couch. But conscience has not to upbraid me with any of these things. I flatter myself that I bear even this patiently; I remember to have often made sleepy but pleasant remarks to the faithful little friend whose affection for me and whose desire to behold my countenance was too great to permit her to wait till breakfast time.

If I lay awake for hours afterward, perhaps getting nothing more than literal "cat-naps," I consoled myself with remembering how Richelieu, and Wellington, and Mohammed, and otherwise great as well as discriminating persons, loved cats; I remembered, with some stirrings of secret pride, that it is only the artistic nature, the truly aesthetic soul that appreciates poetry, and grace, and all refined beauty, who truly loves cats; and thus meditating with closed eyes, I courted slumber again, throughout the breaking dawn, while the cat purred in delight close at hand.

The Pretty Lady was evidently of Angora or coon descent, as her fur was always longer and silkier than that of ordinary cats. She was fond of all the family. When we boarded in Boston, we kept her in a front room, two flights from the ground. Whenever any of us came in the front door, she knew it. No human being could have told, sitting in a closed room in winter, two flights up, the identity of a person coming up the steps and opening the door. But the Pretty Lady, then only six months old, used to rouse from her nap in a big chair, or from the top of a folding bed, jump down, and be at the hall door ready to greet the incomer, before she was halfway up the stairs. The cat never got down for the wrong person, and she never neglected to meet any and every member of our family who might be entering. The irreverent scoffer may call it "instinct," or talk about the "sense of smell." I call it sagacity.

One summer we all went up to the farm in northern Vermont, and decided to take her and her son, "Mr. McGinty," with us. We put them both in a large market-basket and tied the cover securely. On the train Mr. McGinty manifested a desire to get out, and was allowed to do so, a stout cord having been secured to his collar first, and the other end tied to the car seat. He had a delightful journey, once used to the noise and motion of the train. He sat on our laps, curled up on the seat and took naps, or looked out of the windows with evident puzzlement at the way things had suddenly taken to flying; he even made friends with the passengers, and in general amused himself as any other traveller would on an all-day's journey by rail, except that he did not risk his eyesight by reading newspapers. But the Pretty Lady had not travelled for some years, and did not enjoy the trip as well as formerly; on the contrary she curled herself into a round tight ball in one corner of the basket till the journey's end was reached.

Once at the farm she seemed contented as long as I remained with her. There was plenty of milk and cream, and she caught a great many mice. She was far too dainty to eat them, but she had an inherent pleasure in catching mice, just like her more plebeian sisters; and she enjoyed presenting them to Mr. McGinty or me, or some other worthy object of her solicitude.

She was at first afraid of "the big outdoors." The wide, wind-blown spaces, the broad, sunshiny sky, the silence and the roominess of it all, were quite different from her suburban experiences; and the farm animals, too, were in her opinion curiously dangerous objects. Big Dan, the horse, was truly a horrible creature; the rooster was a new and suspicious species of biped, and the bleating calves objects of her direst hatred.

The pig in his pen possessed for her the most horrid fascination. Again and again would she steal out and place herself where she could see that dreadful, strange, pink, fat creature inside his own quarters. She would fix her round eyes widely upon him in blended fear and admiration. If the pig uttered the characteristic grunt of his race, the Pretty Lady at first ran swiftly away; but afterward she used to turn and gaze anxiously at us, as if to say:--

"Do you hear that? Isn't this a truly horrible creature?" and in other ways evince the same sort of surprise that a professor in the Peabody Museum might, were the skeleton of the megatherium suddenly to accost him after the manner peculiar to its kind.

It was funnier, even, to see Mr. McGinty on the morning after his arrival at the farm, as he sallied forth and made acquaintance with other of God's creatures than humans and cats, and the natural enemy of his kind, the dog. In his suburban home he had caught rats and captured on the sly many an English sparrow. When he first investigated his new quarters on the farm, he discovered a beautiful flock of very large birds led by one of truly gorgeous plumage.

"Ah!" thought Mr. McGinty, "this is a great and glorious country, where I can have such birds as these for the catching. Tame, too. I'll have one for breakfast."

So he crouched down, tiger-like, and crept carefully along to a convenient distance and was preparing to spring, when the large and gorgeous bird looked up from his worm and remarked:--

"Cut-cut-cut, ca-dah-cut!" and, taking his wives, withdrew toward the barn.

Mr. McGinty drew back amazed. "This is a queer bird," he seemed to say; "saucy, too. However, I'll soon have him," and he crept more carefully than before up to springing distance, when again this most gorgeous bird drew up and exclaimed, with a note of annoyance:--

"Cut-cut-cut, ca-dah-cut! What ails that old cat, anyway?" And again he led his various wives barn-ward.

Mr. McGinty drew up with a surprised air, and apparently made a cursory study of the leading anatomical features of this strange bird; but he did not like to give up, and soon crouched and prepared for another onslaught. This time Mr. Chanticleer allowed the cat to come up close to his flock, when he turned and remarked in the most amicable manner, "Cut-cut-cut-cut!" which interpreted seemed to mean: "Come now; that's all right. You're evidently new here; but you'd better take my advice and not fool with me."

Anyhow, with this, down went McGinty's hope of a bird breakfast "to the bottom of the sea," and he gave up the hunt. He soon made friends, however, with every animal on the place, and so endeared himself to the owners that he lived out his days there with a hundred acres and more as his own happy hunting-ground.

Not so, the Pretty Lady. I went away on a short visit after a few weeks, leaving her behind. From the moment of my disappearance she was uneasy and unhappy. On the fifth day she disappeared. When I returned and found her not, I am not ashamed to say that I hunted and called her everywhere, nor even that I shed a few tears when days rolled into weeks and she did not appear, as I realized that she might be starving, or have suffered tortures from some larger animal.

There are many remarkable stories of cats who find their way home across almost impossible roads and enormous distances. There is a saying, believed by many people, "You can't lose a cat," which can be proved by hundreds of remarkable returns. But the Pretty Lady had absolutely no sense of locality. She had always lived indoors and had never been allowed to roam the neighborhood. It was five weeks before we found trace of her, and then only by accident. My sister was passing a field of grain, and caught a glimpse of a small creature which she at first thought to be a woodchuck. She turned and looked at it, and called "Pussy, pussy," when with a heart-breaking little cry of utter delight and surprise, our beloved cat came toward her. From the first, the wide expanse of the country had confused her; she had evidently "lost her bearings" and was probably all the time within fifteen minutes' walk of the farm-house.

When found, she was only a shadow of herself, and for the first and only time in her life we could count her ribs. She was wild with delight, and clung to my sister's arms as though fearing to lose her; and in all the fuss that was made over her return, no human being could have showed more affection, or more satisfaction at finding her old friends again.

That she really was lost, and had no sense of locality to guide her home, was proven by her conduct after she returned to her Boston home. I had preceded my sister, and was at the theatre on the evening when she arrived with the Pretty Lady. The latter was carried into the kitchen, taken from her basket, and fed. Then, instead of going around the house and settling herself in her old home, she went into the front hall which she had left four months before, and seated herself on the spot where she always watched and waited when I was out. When I came home at eleven, I saw through the screen door her "that was lost and is found." She had been waiting to welcome me for three mortal hours.

I wish those people who believe cats have no affection for people could have seen her then. She would not leave me for an instant, and manifested her love in every possible way; and when I retired for the night, she curled up on my pillow and purred herself contentedly to sleep, only rising when I did. After breakfast that first morning after her return, she asked to be let out of the back door, and made me understand that I must go with her. I did so, and she explored every part of the back yard, entreating me in the same way she called her kittens to keep close by her. She investigated our own premises thoroughly and then crept carefully under the fences on either side into the neighbor's precincts where she had formerly visited in friendly fashion; then she came timidly back, all the time keeping watch that she did not lose me. Having finished her tour of inspection, she went in and led me on an investigating trip all through the house, smelling of every corner and base-board, and insisting that every closet door should be opened, so that she might smell each closet through in the same way. When this was done, she settled herself in one of her old nooks for a nap and allowed me to leave.

But never again did she go out of sight of the house. For more than a year she would not go even into a neighbor's yard, and when she finally decided that it might be safe to crawl under the fences on to other territory, she invariably turned about to sit facing the house, as though living up to a firm determination never to lose sight of it again. This practice she kept up until at the close of her last mortal sickness, when she crawled into a dark place under a neighboring barn and said good-by to earthly fears and worries forever.

Requiescat in pace, my Pretty Lady. I wish all your sex had your gentle dignity, and grace, and beauty, to say nothing of your faithfulness and affection. Like Mother Michel's "Monmouth," it may be said of you:--

"She was merely a cat,
But her Sublime Virtues place her on a level with
The Most Celebrated Mortals,
and
In Ancient Egypt
Altars would have been Erected to her
Memory."

CHAPTER II
CONCERNING MY OTHER CATS

O h, what a lovely cat!" is a frequent expression from visitors or passers-by at our house. And from the Pretty Lady down through her various sons and daughters to the present family protector and head, "Thomas Erastus," and the Angora, "Lady Betty," there have been some beautiful creatures.

Mr. McGinty was a solid-color maltese, with fur like a seal for closeness and softness, and with the disposition of an angel. He used to be seized with sudden spasms of affection and run from one to another of the family, rubbing his soft cheeks against ours, and kissing us repeatedly. This he did by taking gentle little affectionate nips with his teeth. I used to give him a certain caress, which he took as an expression of affection. After leaving him at the farm I did not see him again for two years. Then on a short visit, I asked for Mr. McGinty and was told that he was in a shed chamber. I found him asleep in a box of grain and took him out; he looked at me through sleepy eyes, turned himself over and stretched up for the old caress. As nobody ever gave him that but me, I take this as conclusive proof that he not only knew me, but remembered my one peculiarity.

Then there was old Pomp, called "old" to distinguish him from the young Pomp of to-day, or "Pompanita." He died of pneumonia at the age of three years; but he was the handsomest black cat--and the blackest--I have ever seen. He had half a dozen white hairs under his chin; but his blackness was literally like the raven's wing. Many handsome black cats show brown in the strong sunlight, or when their fur is parted. But old Pomp's fur was jet black clear through, and in the sunshine looked as if he had been made up of the richest black silk velvet, his eyes, mean-while, being large and of the purest amber. He weighed some fifteen pounds, and that somebody envied us the possession of him was evident, as he was stolen two or three times during the last summer of his life. But he came home every time; only when Death finally stole him, we had no redress.

"Bobinette," the black kitten referred to in the previous chapter, also had remarkably beautiful eyes. We used to keep him in ribbons to match, and he knew color, too, perfectly well. For instance, if we offered him a blue or a red ribbon, he would not be quiet long enough to have it tied on; but show him a yellow one, and he would prance across the room, and not only stand still to have it put on, but purr and evince the greatest pride in it.

Bobinette had another very pretty trick of playing with the tape-measure. He used to bring it to us and have it wound several times around his body; then he would "chase himself" until he got it off, when he would bring it back and ask plainly to have it wound round him again. After a little we noticed he was wearing the tape-measure out, and so we tried to substitute it with an old ribbon or piece of cotton tape. But Bobinette would have none of them. On the contrary, he repeatedly climbed on to the table and to the work-basket, and hunted patiently for his tape-measure, and even if it were hidden in a pocket, he kept up the search until he unearthed it; and he would invariably end by dragging forth that particular tape-measure and bringing it to us. I need not say that his intelligence was rewarded.

Speaking of colors, a friend has a cat that is devoted to blue. When she puts on a particularly pretty blue gown, the cat hastens to get into her lap, put her face down to the material, purr, and manifest the greatest delight; but let the same lady put on a black dress, and the cat will not come near her.

"Pompanita," the second Pomp in our dynasty, is a fat and billowy black fellow, now five years old and weighing nineteen pounds. He was the last of the Pretty Lady's ninety-three children. Only a few of this vast progeny, however, grew to cat-hood, as she was never allowed to keep more than one each season. The Pretty Lady, in fact, came to regard this as the only proper method. On one occasion I had been away all day. When I got home at night the housekeeper said, "Pussy has had five kittens, but she won't go near them." When the Pretty Lady heard my voice, she came and led the way to the back room where the kittens were in the lower drawer of an unused bureau, and uttered one or two funny little noises, intimating that matters were not altogether as they should be, according to established rules of propriety. I understood, abstracted four of the five kittens, and disappeared. When I came back she had settled herself contentedly with the remaining kitten, and from that time on was a model mother.

Pompanita the Good has all the virtues of a good cat, and absolutely no vices. He loves us all and loves all other cats as well. As for fighting, he emulates the example of that veteran who boasts that during the war he might always be found where the shot and shell were the thickest,--under the ammunition wagon. Like most cats he has a decided streak of vanity. My sister cut a wide, fancy collar, or ruff, of white paper one day, and put it on Pompanita. At first he felt much abashed and found it almost impossible to walk with it. But a few words of praise and encouragement changed all that.

"Oh, what a pretty Pomp he is now!" exclaimed one and another, until he sat up coyly and cocked his head one side as if to say:--

"Oh, now, do you really think I look pretty?" and after a few more assurances he got down and strutted as proudly as any peacock; much to the discomfiture of the kitten, who wanted to play with him. And now he will cross the yard any time to have one of those collars on.

But Thomas Erastus is the prince of our cats to-day. He weighs seventeen pounds, and is a soft, grayish-maltese with white paws and breast. One Saturday night ten years ago, as we were partaking of our regular Boston baked beans, I heard a faint mew. Looking down I saw beside me the thinnest kitten I ever beheld. The Irish girl who presided over our fortunes at the time used to place the palms of her hands together and say of Thomas's appearance, "Why, mum, the two sides of 'im were just like that." I picked him up, and he crawled pathetically into my neck and cuddled down.

"There," said a friend who was sitting opposite, "he's fixed himself now. You'll keep him."

"No, I shall not," I said, "but I will feed him a few days and give him to my cousin." Inside half an hour, however, Thomas Erastus had assumed the paternal air toward us that soon made us fear to lose him. Living without Thomas now would be like a young girl's going out without a chaperone. After that first half-hour, when he had been fed, he chased every foreign cat off the premises, and assumed the part of a watch-dog. To this day he will sit on the front porch or the window-sill and growl if he sees a tramp or suspicious character approaching. He always goes into the kitchen when the market-man calls, and orders his meat; and at exactly five o'clock in the afternoon, when the meat is cut up and distributed, leads the feline portion of the family into the kitchen.

Thomas knows the time of day. For six months he waked up one housekeeper at exactly seven o'clock in the morning, never varying two minutes. He did this by seating himself on her chest and gazing steadfastly in her face. Usually this waked her, but if she did not yield promptly to that treatment he would poke her cheeks with the most velvety of paws until she awoke. He has a habit now of going upstairs and sitting opposite the closed door of the young man who has to rise hours before the rest of us do, and waiting until the door is opened for him. How he knows at what particular moment each member of the family will wake up and come forth is a mystery, but he does.

How do cats tell the hour of day, anyway? The old Chinese theory that they are living clocks is, in a way, borne out by their own conduct. Not only have my cats shown repeatedly that they know the hour of rising of every member of the family, but they gather with as much regularity as the ebbing of the tides, or the setting of the sun, at exactly five o'clock in the afternoon for their supper. They are given a hearty breakfast as soon as the kitchen fire is started in the morning. This theoretically lasts them until five. I say theoretically, because if they wake from their invariable naps at one, and smell lunch, they individually wheedle some one into feeding them. But this is only individually. Collectively they are fed at five.

They are the most methodical creatures in the world. They go to bed regularly at night when the family does. They are waiting in the kitchen for breakfast when the fire is started in the morning. Then they go out of doors and play, or hunt, or ruminate until ten o'clock, when they come in, seek their favorite resting-places, and sleep until four. Evidently, from four to five is a play hour, and the one who wakes first is expected to stir up the others. But at exactly five, no matter where they may have strayed to, every one of the three, five, or seven (as the number may happen to be) will be sitting in his own particular place in the kitchen, waiting with patient eagerness for supper. For each has a particular place for eating, just as bigger folk have their places at the dining table. Thomas Erastus sits in a corner; the space under the table is reserved especially for Jane. Pompanita is at his mistress's feet, and Lady Betty, the Angora, bounds to her shoulder when their meat appears. Their table manners are quite irreproachable also. It is considered quite unpardonable to snatch at another's piece of meat, and a breach of the best cat-etiquette to show impatience while another is being fed.

I do not pretend to say that this is entirely natural. They are taught these things as kittens, and since cats are as great sticklers for propriety and gentle manners as any human beings can be, they never forget it. Doubtless, this is easier because they are always well fed, but Thomas Erastus or Jane would have to be on the verge of starvation, I am sure, before they would "grab" from one of the other cats. And as for the Pretty Lady, it was always necessary to see that she was properly served. She would not eat from a dish with other cats, or, except in extreme cases, from one they had left. Indeed, she was remarkable in this respect. I have seen her sit on the edge of a table where chickens were being dressed and wait patiently for a tidbit; I have seen her left alone in the room, while on that table was a piece of raw steak, but no temptation was ever great enough to make her touch any of these forbidden things. She actually seemed to have a conscience.

Only one thing on the dining table would she touch. When she was two or three months old, she somehow got hold of the table-napkins done up in their rings. These were always to her the most delightful playthings in the world. As a kitten, she would play with them by the hour, if not taken away, and go to sleep cuddled affectionately around them. She got over this as she grew older; but when her first kitten was two or three months old, remembering the jolly times she used to have, she would sneak into the dining room and get the rolled napkins, carry them in her mouth to her infant, and endeavor with patient anxiety to show him how to play with them. Throughout nine years of motherhood she went through the same performance with every kitten she had. They never knew what to do with the napkins, or cared to know, and would have none of them. But she never got discouraged. She would climb up on the sideboard, or into the china closet, and even try to get into drawers where the napkins were laid away in their rings. If she could get hold of one, she would carry it with literal groans and evident travail of spirit to her kitten, and by further groans and admonitions seem to say:--

"Child, see this beautiful plaything I have brought you. This is a part of your education; it is just as necessary for you to know how to play with this as to poke your paw under the closet door properly. Wake up, now, and play with it."

Sometimes, when the table was laid over night, we used to hear her anguished groans in the stillness of the night. In the morning every napkin belonging to the family would be found in a different part of the house, and perhaps a ring would be missing. These periods, however, only lasted as long, in each new kitten's training, as the few weeks that she had amused herself with them at their age. Then she would drop the subject, and napkins had no further interest than the man in the moon until another kitten arrived at the age when she considered them a necessary part of his education.

Professor Shaler in his interesting book on the intelligence of animals gives the cat only the merest mention, intimating that he considers them below par in this respect, and showing little real knowledge of them. I wish he might have known the Pretty Lady.

Once our Lady Betty had four little Angora kittens. She was probably the most aristocratic cat in the country, for she kept a wet nurse. Poor Jane, of commoner strain, had two small kittens the day after the Angora family appeared. Jane's plebeian infants promptly disappeared, but she took just as promptly to the more aristocratic family and fulfilled the duties of nurse and maid. Both cats and four kittens occupied the same bureau drawer, and when either cat wanted the fresh air she left the other in charge; and there was a tacit understanding between them that the fluffy, fat babies must never be left alone one instant. Four small and lively kittens in the house are indeed things of beauty, and a joy as long as they last. Four fluffy little Angora balls they were Chin, Chilla, Buffie, and Orange Pekoe, names that explain their color. And Jane, wet nurse and waiting-maid, had to keep as busy as the old woman that lived in a shoe. Jane it was who must look after the infants when Lady Betty wished to leave the house. Jane it was who must scrub the furry quartet until their silky fur stood up in bunches the wrong way all over their chubby little sides; Jane must sleep with them nights, and be ready to furnish sustenance at any moment of day or night; and above all, Jane must watch them anxiously and incessantly in waking hours, uttering those little protesting murmurs of admonition which mother cats deem so necessary toward the proper training of kittens. And, poor Jane! As lady's maid she must bathe Lady Betty's brow every now and then, as the more finely strung Angora succumbed to the nervous strain of kitten-rearing, and she turned affectionately to Jane for comfort. A prettier sight, or a more profitable study of the love of animals for each other was never seen than Lady Betty, her infants, and her nurse-maid. And yet, there are people who pronounce cats stupid.

One evening I returned from the theatre late and roused up the four fluffy kittens, who, seeing the gas turned on, started in for a frolic. The lady mother did not approve of midnight carousals on the part of infants, and protested with mild wails against their joyful caperings. Finally, Orange Pekoe got into the closet and Lady Betty pursued him. But suddenly a strange odor was detected. Sitting on her haunches she smelled all over the bottom of the skirt which had just been hung up, stopping every few seconds to utter a little worried note of warning to the kittens. The infants, however, displayed a quite human disregard of parental authority and gambolled on unconcernedly under the skirt; reminding one of the old New England primer style of tales, showing how disobedient children flaunt themselves in the face of danger, despite the judicious advice of their elders. Lady Betty could do nothing with them, and grew more nervous and worried every minute in consequence. Suddenly she bethought herself of that never-failing source of strength and comfort, Jane. She went into the next room, and, although I had not heard a sound, returned in a moment with the maltese. Jane was ushered into the closet, and soon scented out the skirt. Then she too sat on her haunches and gave a long, careful sniff, turned round and uttered one "purr-t-t," and took the Angora off with her. Jane had discovered that there was no element of danger in the closet, and had imparted her knowledge to the finely strung Angora in an instant. And so, taking her back to bed, she "bathed her brow" with gentle lappings until Lady Betty sank off to quiet sleep, soothed and comforted.

It is not easy to study a cat. They are like sensitive plants, and shut themselves instinctively away from the human being who does not care for them. They know when a man or a woman loves them, almost before they come into the human presence; and it is almost useless for the unsympathetic person to try to study a cat. But the thousands who do love cats know that they are the most individual animals in the world. Dogs are much alike in their love for mankind, their obedience, faithfulness, and, in different degrees, their sagacity. But there is as much individuality in cats as in people.

Dogs and horses are our slaves; cats never. This does not prove them without affection, as some people seem to think; on the contrary, it proves their peculiar and characteristic dignity and self-respect. Women, poets, and especially artists, like cats; delicate natures only can realize their sensitive nervous systems.

The Pretty Lady's mother talked almost incessantly when she was in the house. One of her habits was to get on the window-seat outside and demand to be let in. If she was not waited upon immediately, she would, when the door was finally opened, stop when halfway in and scold vigorously. The tones of her voice and the expression of her face were so exactly like those of a scolding, vixenish woman that she caused many a hearty laugh by her tirades.

Thomas Erastus, however, seldom utters a sound, and at the rare intervals when he condescends to purr, he can only be heard by holding one's ear close to his great, soft sides. But he has the most remarkable ways. He will open every door in the house from the inside; he will even open blinds, getting his paw under the fastening and working patiently at it, with his body on the blind itself, until the hook flies back and it finally opens. One housekeeper trained him to eat his meat close up in one corner of the kitchen. This custom he kept up after she went away, until new and uncommonly frisky kittens annoyed him so that his place was transferred to the top of an old table. When he got hungry in those days, however, he used to go and crowd close up in his corner and look so pathetically famished that food was generally forthcoming at once. Thomas was formerly very much devoted to the lady who lived next door, and was as much at home in her house as in ours. Her family rose an hour or two earlier than ours in the morning, and their breakfast hour came first. I should attribute Thomas's devotion to Mrs. T. to this fact, since he invariably presented himself at her dining-room window and wheedled her into feeding him, were it not that his affection seemed just as strong throughout the day. It was interesting to see him go over and rattle her screen doors, front, back, or side, knowing perfectly well that he would bring some one to open and let him in.

Thomas has a really paternal air toward the rest of the family. One spring night, as usual on retiring, I went to the back door to call in the cats. Thomas Erastus was in my sister's room, but none of the others were to be seen; nor did they come at once, evidently having strayed in their play beyond the sound of my voice. Thomas, upstairs, heard my continued call and tried for some time to get out. M. had shut her door, thinking to keep in the one already safe. But the more I called, the more persistently determined he became to get out. At last M. opened her window and let him on to the sloping roof of the "L," from which he could descend through a gnarled old apple tree. Meanwhile I left the back door and went on with my preparations for the night. About ten minutes later I went and called the cats again. It was a moonlight night and I saw six delinquent cats coming in a flock across the open field behind the house,--all marshalled by Mr. Thomas. He evidently hunted them up and called them in himself; then he sat on the back porch and waited until the last kit was safely in, before he stalked gravely in with an air which said as plainly as words:--

"There, it takes *me* to do anything with this family."

None of my cats would think of responding to the call of "Kitty, Kitty," or "Puss, Puss." They are early taught their names and answer to them. Neither would one answer to the name of another, except in occasional instances where jealousy prompts them to do so. We have to be most careful when we go out of an evening, not to let Thomas Erastus get out at the same time. In case he does, he will follow us either to the railroad station or to the electric cars and wait in some near-by nook until we come back. I have known him to sit out from seven until midnight of a cold, snowy winter evening, awaiting our return from the theatre. When we alight from the cars he is nowhere to be seen. But before we have gone many steps, lo! Thomas Erastus is behind or beside us, proudly escorting his mistresses home, but looking neither at them, nor to the right or left. Not until he reaches the porch does he allow himself to be petted. But on our way to the cars his attitude is different. He is as frisky as a kitten. In vain do we try to "shoo" him back, or catch him. He prances along, just out of reach, but tantalizingly close; when we get aboard our car, we know he is safe in some corner gazing sadly after us, and that no danger can drive him home until we reappear.

Both Thomas and Pompanita take a deep interest in all household affairs, although in this respect they do not begin to show the curiosity of the Pretty Lady. Never a piece of furniture was changed in he house that she did not immediately notice, the first time she came into the room afterward; and she invariably jumped up on the article and thoroughly investigated affairs before settling down again. Every parcel that came in must be examined, and afterward she must lie on the paper or inside the box that it came in, always doing this with great solemnity and gazing earnestly out of her large, intelligent dark eyes. Toward the close of her life she was greatly troubled at any unusual stir in the household. She liked to have company, but nothing disturbed her more than to have a man working in the cellar, putting in coal, cutting wood, or doing such work. She used then to follow us uneasily about and look earnestly up into our faces, as if to say:--

"Girls, this is not right. Everything is all upset here and 'a' the world's gang agley.' Why don't you fix it?"

She was the politest creature, too. That was the reason of her name. In her youth she was christened "Pansy"; then "Cleopatra," "Susan," "Lady Jane Grey" and the "Duchess." But her manners were so punctiliously perfect, and she was such a "pretty lady" always and everywhere; moreover she had such a habit of sitting with her hands folded politely across her gentle, lace-vandyked bosom that the only so-briquet that ever clung was the one that expressed herself the most perfectly. She was in every sense a "Pretty Lady." For years she ate with us at the table. Her chair was placed next to mine, and no matter where she was or how soundly she had been sleeping, when the dinner bell rang she was the first to get to her seat. Then she sat patiently until I fixed a dainty meal in a saucer and placed it in the chair beside her, when she ate it in the same well-bred way she did everything.

Thomas Erastus hurt his foot one day. Rather he got it hurt during a matutinal combat at which he was forced, being the head of the family, to be present, although he is far above the midnight carousals of his kind. Thomas Erastus sometimes loves to consider himself an invalid. When his doting mistress was not looking, he managed to step off on that foot quite lively, especially if his mortal enemy, a disreputable black tramp, skulked across the yard. But let Thomas Erastus see a feminine eye gazing anxiously at him through an open window, and he immediately hobbled on three legs; then he would stop and sit down and assume so pathetic an expression of patient suffering that the mistress's heart would melt, and Thomas Erastus would find himself being borne into the house and placed on the softest sofa. Once she caught him down cellar. There is a window to which he has easy access, and where he can go in and out a hundred times a day. Evidently he had planned to do so at that moment. But seeing his fond mistress, he sat down on the cellar floor, and with his most fetching expression gazed wistfully back and forth from her to the window. And of course she picked him up carefully and put him on the window ledge. Thomas Erastus has all the innocent guile of a successful politician. He could manage things slicker than the political bosses, an' he would.

One summer Thomas Erastus moved--an event of considerable importance in his placid existence. He had to travel a short distance on the steam-cars; and worse, he needs must endure the indignity of travelling that distance in a covered basket. But his dignity would not suffer him to do more than send forth one or two mournful wails of protest. After being kept in his new house for a couple of days, he was allowed to go out and become familiar with his surroundings--not without fear and trepidation on the part of his doting mistress that he might make a bold strike for his former home. But Thomas Erastus felt he had a mission to perform for his race. He would disprove that mistaken theory that a cat, no matter how kindly he is treated, cares more for places than for people. Consequently he would not dream of going back to his old haunts.

No; he sat down in the front yard and took a long look at his surroundings, the neighboring lots, a field of grass, a waving corn-field. He had already convinced himself that the new house was home, because in it were all the old familiar things, and he had been allowed to investigate every bit of it and to realize what had happened. So after looking well about him he made a series of tours of investigation. First, he took a bee-line for the farthest end of the nearest vacant lot; then he chose the corn-field; then the beautiful broad grounds of the neighbor below; then across the street; but between each of these little journeys he took a bee-line back to his starting-point, sat down in front of the new house, and "got his bearings," just as evidently as though he could have said out loud, "This is my home and I mustn't lose it." In this way he convinced himself that where he lives is the centre of the universe, and that the world revolves around him. And he has since been as happy as a cricket,--yea, happier, for death and destruction await the unfortunate cricket where Thomas Erastus thrives.

But don't say a cat can't or won't be moved. It's your own fault if he won't.

CHAPTER III
CONCERNING OTHER PEOPLE'S CATS

Every observing reader of Mrs. Harriet Prescott Spofford's stories knows that she is fond of cats and understands them. Her heroines usually have, among other feminine belongings and accessories, one or more cats. "Four great Persian cats haunted her every footstep," she says of Honor, in the "Composite Wife." "A sleepy, snowy creature like some half-animated ostrich plume; a satanic thing with fiery eyes that to Mr. Chipperley's perception were informed with the very bottomless flames; another like a golden fleece, caressing, half human; and a little mouse-colored imp whose bounds and springs and feathery tail-lashings not only did infinite damage among the Venetian and Dresden knick-knackerie, but among Mr. Chipperley's nerves."

In her beautiful, old-fashioned home at Newburyport, Mass., she has two beloved cats. But I will not attempt to improve on her own account of them:--

"As for my own cats,--their name has been legion, although a few remain pre-eminent. There was Miss Spot who came to us already named, preferring our domicile to the neighboring one she had. Her only son was so black that he was known as Ink Spot, but her only daughter was so altogether ideal and black, too, that she was known as Beauty Spot. Beauty Spot led a sorrowful life, and was fortunately born clothed in black or her mourning would have been expensive, as she was always in a bereaved condition, her drowned offspring making a shoal in the Merrimac, although she had always plenty left. She solaced herself with music. She would never sit in any one's lap but mine, and in mine only when I sang; and then only when I sang 'The Last Rose of Summer.' This is really true. But she would spring into my husband's lap if he whistled. She would leave her sleep reluctantly, start a little way, and retreat, start and retreat again, and then give one bound and light on his knee or his arm and reach up one paw and push it repeatedly across his mouth like one playing the jew's-harp; I suppose to get at the sound. She always went to walk with us and followed us wherever we went about the island.

"Lucifer and Phosphor have been our cats for the last ten years: Lucifer, entirely black, Phosphor, as yellow as saffron, a real golden fleece. My sister lived in town and going away for the summer left her cat in a neighbor's care, and the neighbor moved away meanwhile and left the cat to shift for herself. She went down to the apothecary's, two blocks away or more. There she had a family of kittens, but apparently came up to reconnoitre, for on my sister's return, she appeared with one kitten and laid it down at Kate's feet; ran off, and in time came with another which she left also, and so on until she had brought up the whole household. Lucifer was one of them.

"He was as black as an imp and as mischievous as one. His bounds have always been tremendous: from the floor to the high mantel, or to the top of a tall buffet close under the ceiling. And these bounds of his, together with a way he has of gazing into space with his soulful and enormous yellow eyes, have led to a thousand tales as to his nightly journeyings among the stars; hurting his foot slumping through the nebula in Andromeda; getting his supper at a place in the milky way, hunting all night with Orion, and having awful fights with Sirius. He got his throat cut by alighting on the North Pole one night, coming down from the stars. The reason he slumps through the nebula is on account of his big feet; he has six toes (like the foot in George Augustus Sala's drawing) and when he walks on the top of the piazza you would think it was a burglar.

"Lucifer's Mephistophelian aspect is increased not only by those feet, but by an arrow-pointed tail. He sucks his tail,--alas, and alas! In vain have we peppered it, and pepper-sauced it, and dipped it in Worcestershire sauce and in aloes, and done it up in curl papers, and glued on it the fingers of old gloves. At last we gave it up in despair, and I took him and put his tail in his mouth and told him to take his pleasure,--and that is the reason, I suppose, that he attaches himself particularly to me. He is very near-sighted with those magnificent orbs, for he will jump into any one's lap, who wears a black gown, but jump down instantly, and when he finds my lap curl down for a brief season. But he is not much of a lap-loving cat. He puts up his nose and smells my face all over in what he means for a caress, and is off. He is not a large eater, although he has been known to help himself to a whole steak at the table, being alone in the dining room; and when poultry are in the larder he is insistent till satisfied. But he wants his breakfast early. If the second girl, whose charge he is, does not rise in season, he mounts two flights of stairs and seats himself on her chest until she does rise. Then if she does not wait on him at once, he goes into the drawing-room, and springs to the top of the upright piano, and deliberately knocks off the bric-a-brac, particularly loving to encounter and floor a brass dragon candlestick. Then he springs to the mantel-shelf if he has not been seized and appeased, and repeats operations, and has even carried his work of destruction around the room to the top of a low bookcase and has proved himself altogether the wrong sort of person in a china-shop.

"However, it is conceded in the family that Phosphor is not a cat merely: he is a person, and Lucifer is a spirit. Lucifer seldom purrs--I wonder if that is a characteristic of black cats?" [No; my black cats fairly roar.] "A little thread of sound, and only now and then, when very happy and loving, a rich, full strain. But Phosphor purrs like a windmill, like an electric car, like a tea-kettle, like a whole boiled dinner. When Phosphor came, Lucifer, six weeks her senior (Phosphor's excellencies always incline one to say 'she' of him), thought the little live yellow ball was made only for him to play with, and he cuffed and tossed him around for all he was worth, licked him all over twenty times a day, and slept with his arms about him. During those early years Phosphor never washed himself, Lucifer took such care of him, and they were a lovely sight in each other's arms asleep. But of late years a coolness has intervened, and now they never speak as they pass by. They sometimes go fishing together, Lucifer walking off majestically alone, always dark, mysterious, reticent, intent on his own affairs, making you feel that he has a sort of lofty contempt for yours. Sometimes, the mice depositing a dead fish in the crannies of the rocks, Lucifer appears with it in the twilight, gleaming silver-white in his jaws, and the great eyes gleaming like fire-balls above it. Phosphor is, however, a mighty hunter: mice, rats by the score, chipmunks,--all is game that comes to his net. He has cleaned out whole colonies of catbirds (for their insolence), and eaten every golden robin on the island.

"It used to be very pretty to see them, when they were little, as El Mahdi, the peacock, spread his great tail, dart and spring upon it, and go whirling round with it as El Mahdi, fairly frantic with the little demons that had hold of him, went skipping and springing round and round. But although so fierce a fighter, so inhospitable to every other cat, Phosphor is the most affectionate little soul. He is still very playful, though so large, and last summer to see him bounding on the grass, playing with his tail, turning somersaults all by himself, was quite worth while. When we first happened to go away in his early years he wouldn't speak to us when we came back, he felt so neglected. I went away for five months once, before Lucifer was more than a year old. He got into no one's lap while I was gone, but the moment I sat down on my return, he jumped into mine, saluted me, and curled himself down for a nap, showing the plainest recognition. Now when one comes back, Phosphor is wild with joy--always in a well-bred way. He will get into your arms and on your shoulder and rub his face around, and before you know it his little mouth is in the middle of your mouth as much like a kiss as anything can be. Perhaps it isn't so well bred, but his motions are so quick and perfect it seems so. When you let him in he curls into heaps of joy, and fairly stands on his head sometimes. He is the most responsive creature, always ready for a caress, and his wild, great amber eyes beam love, if ever love had manifestation. His beauty is really extraordinary; his tail a real wonder. Lucifer, I grieve to say, looks very moth-eaten. Phosphor wore a bell for a short time once--a little Inch-Cape Rock bell--but he left it to toll all winter in a tall tree near the drawing-room window.

"A charm of cats is that they seem to live in a world of their own, just as much as if it were a real dimension of space; and speaking of a fourth dimension, I am living in the expectation that the new discoveries in the matter of radiant energy will presently be revealing to all our senses the fact that there is no death.

"We had some barn kittens once that lived in the hen-house, ate with the hens, and quarrelled with them for any tidbit. They curled up in the egg boxes and didn't move when the hens came to lay, and evidently had no idea that they were not hens.

"Oh, there is no end to the cat situation. It began with the old fellow who put his hand under the cat to lift her up, and she arched her back higher and higher until he found it was the serpent Asgard, and it won't end with you and me. I don't know but she *is* the serpent Asgard. I don't know if you have hypnotized or magnetized me, but I am writing as if I had known you intimately all my life, and feel as though I had. It is the freemasonry of cats. I always said they were possessed of spirits, and they use white magic to bring their friends together."

Mrs. Spofford's "barn kittens" bring to mind an incident related by Mrs. Wood, the beautiful wife of Professor C.G. Wood, of the Harvard Medical School. At their summer place on Buzzard's Bay she has fifteen cats, mostly Angoras, Persians, and coons, with several dogs. These cats follow her all about the place in a regular troop, and a very handsome troop they are, with their waving, plumy tails tipped gracefully over at the ends as if saluting their superior officer. Among the dogs is a spaniel named Gyp that is particularly friendly with the cats. There are plenty of hens on the farm, and one spring a couple of bantams were added to the stock. The cats immediately took a great fancy to these diminutive bipeds, and watched them with the greatest interest. Finally the little hen had a flock of chickens. As the weather was still cold, the farmer put them upstairs in one of the barns, and every day Gyp would take seven or eight of those cats up there to see the fluffy little things. Dog and cats would seat themselves around the bantam and her brood and watch them by the hour, never offering to touch the chickens except when the little things were tired and went for a nap under their mother's wings; and then some cat--first one and then another--would softly poke its paw under the hen and stir up the family, making them all run out in consternation, and keeping things lively once more. The cats didn't dream of catching the chickens, only wanting, evidently, that they should emulate Joey and keep moving on.

A writer in the ***London Spectator*** tells of a favorite bantam hen with which the house cat has long been accustomed to play. This bantam has increased and multiplied, and keeps her family in a "coop" on the ground,--into which rats easily enter. At bedtime, however, pussy takes up her residence there, and bantam, the brood of chickens, and pussy sleep in happy harmony nightly. If any rats arrive, their experience must be sad and sharp. Another writer in the same number tells of a cat in Huddersfield, England, belonging to Canon Beardsley, who helps himself to a reel of cotton from the work-basket, takes it on the floor, and plays with it as long as he likes, and then jumps up and puts the reel back in its place again; just as our Bobinette used to get his tape-measure, although the latter never was known to put it away.

Miss Sarah Orne Jewett is a cat-lover, too, and the dear old countrywomen "down in Maine," with whom one gets acquainted through her books, usually keep a cat also. Says she:--

"I look back over so long a line of family cats, from a certain poor Spotty who died an awful death in a fit on the flagstones under the library window when I was less than five years old, to a lawless, fluffy, yellow and white coon cat now in my possession, that I find it hard to single out the most interesting pussy of all. I shall have to speak of two cats at least, one being the enemy and the other the friend of my dog Joe. Joe and I grew up together and were fond companions, until he died of far too early old age and left me to take my country walks alone.

"Polly, the enemy, was the best mouser of all: quite the best business cat we ever had, with an astonishing intellect and a shrewd way of gaining her ends. She caught birds and mice as if she foraged for our whole family: she had an air of responsibility and a certain impatience of interruption and interference such as I have never seen in any other cat, and a scornful way of sitting before a person with fierce eyes and a quick, ominous twitching of her tail. She seemed to be measuring one's incompetence as a mouse-catcher in these moments, or to be saying to herself, 'What a clumsy, stupid person; how little she knows, and how I should like to scratch her and hear her squeak.' I sometimes felt as if I were a larger sort of helpless mouse in these moments, but sometimes Polly would be more friendly, and even jump into our laps, when it was a pleasure to pat her hard little head with its exquisitely soft, dark tortoise-shell fur. No matter if she almost always turned and caught the caressing hand with teeth and claws, when she was tired of its touch, you would always be ready to pat her next time; there was such a fascination about her that any attention on her part gave a thrill of pride and pleasure. Every guest and stranger admired her and tried to win her favor: while we of the household hid our wounds and delighted in her cleverness and beauty.

"Polly was but a small cat to have a mind. She looked quite round and kittenish as she sat before the fire in a rare moment of leisure, with her black paws tucked under her white breast and her sleek back looking as if it caught flickers of firelight in some yellow streaks among the shiny black fur. But when she walked abroad she stretched out long and thin like a little tiger, and held her head high to look over the grass as if she were threading the jungle. She lashed her tail to and fro, and one turned out of her way instantly. You opened a door for her if she crossed the room and gave you a look. She made you know what she meant as if she had the gift of speech: at most inconvenient moments you would go out through the house to find her a bit of fish or to open the cellar door. You recognized her right to appear at night on your bed with one of her long-suffering kittens, which she had brought in the rain, out of a cellar window and up a lofty ladder, over the wet, steep roofs and down through a scuttle into the garret, and still down into warm shelter. Here she would leave it and with one or two loud, admonishing purrs would scurry away upon some errand that must have been like one of the border frays of old.

"She used to treat Joe, the dog, with sad cruelty, giving him a sharp blow on his honest nose that made him meekly stand back and see her add his supper to her own. A child visitor once rightly complained that Polly had pins in her toes, and nobody knew this better than poor Joe. At last, in despair, he sought revenge. I was writing at my desk one day, when he suddenly appeared, grinning in a funny way he had, and wagging his tail, until he enticed me out to the kitchen. There I found Polly, who had an air of calling everything in the house her own. She was on the cook's table, gobbling away at some chickens which were being made ready for the oven and had been left unguarded. I caught her and cuffed her, and she fled through the garden door, for once tamed and vanquished, though usually she was so quick that nobody could administer justice upon these depredations of a well-fed cat. Then I turned and saw poor old Joe dancing about the kitchen in perfect delight. He had been afraid to touch Polly himself, but he knew the difference between right and wrong, and had called me to see what a wicked cat she was, and to give him the joy of looking on at the flogging.

"It was the same dog who used sometimes to be found under a table where his master had sent him for punishment in his young days of lawless puppy-hood for chasing the neighbor's chickens. These faults had long been overcome, but sometimes, in later years, Joe's conscience would trouble him, we never knew why, and he would go under the table of his own accord, and look repentant and crestfallen until some forgiving and sympathetic friend would think he had suffered enough and bid him come out to be patted and consoled.

"After such a house-mate as Polly, Joe had great amends in our next cat, yellow Danny, the most amiable and friendly pussy that ever walked on four paws. He took Danny to his heart at once: they used to lie in the sun together with Danny's head on the dog's big paws, and I sometimes used to meet them walking as coy as lovers, side by side, up one of the garden walks. When I could not help laughing at their sentimental and conscious air, they would turn aside into the bushes for shelter. They respected each other's suppers, and ate together on the kitchen hearth, and took great comfort in close companionship. Danny always answered if you spoke to him, but he made no sound while always opening his mouth wide to mew whenever he had anything to say, and looking up into your face with all his heart expressed. These affectations of speech were most amusing, especially in so large a person as yellow Danny. He was much beloved by me and by all his family, especially poor Joe, who must sometimes have had the worst of dreams about old Polly, and her sharp, unsparing claws."

Miss Mary E. Wilkins is also a great admirer of cats. "I adore cats," she says. "I don't love them as well as dogs, because my own nature is more after the lines of a dog's; but I adore them. No matter how tired or wretched I am, a pussy-cat sitting in a doorway can divert my mind. Cats love one so much: more than they will allow; but they have so much wisdom they keep it to themselves."

Miss Wilkins's "Augustus" was moved with her from Brattleboro, Vt., after her father's death and when she went to Randolph, Mass., to live. He had been the pet of the family for a long time, but he came to an untimely end.

"I hope," says Miss Wilkins, "people's unintentional cruelty will not be remembered against them." Since living in Randolph she has had two lovely yellow and white cats, "Punch and Judy." The latter was shot by a neighbor, but Punch, the right-hand cat with the angelic expression, still survives.

"I am quite sure," says his mistress, "he loves me better than anybody else, although he is so very close about it. Punch Wilkins has one accomplishment. He can open a door with an old-fashioned latch: but he cannot shut it."

Louise Imogen Guiney is famous for her love and good comradeship with dogs, especially her setters and St. Bernards, but she is too thoroughly a poet not to be captivated by the grace and beauty of a cat.

"I love the unsubmissive race," she says, "and have had much edification out of the charming friendships between our St. Bernards and our cats. Annie Clarke [the actress] once gave me two exquisite Angoras, little persons of character equal to their looks; but they died young and we have not since had the heart to replace them. I once had another coon, a small, spry, gray fellow named Scot, the tamest and most endearing of pets, always on your shoulder and a' that, who suddenly, on no provocation whatever, turned wild, lived for a year or more in the woods next our garden, hunting and fishing, although ceaselessly chased, and called, and implored to revisit his afflicted family. He associated sometimes with the neighbor's cat, but never, never more with humanity, until finally we found his pathetic little frozen body one Christmas near the barn. Do you remember Arnold's Scholar Gypsy? Our Scot was his feline equivalent.... Have you counted in Prosper Merimee among the confirmed lovers of cats? I remember a delightful little paragraph out of one of his letters about *un vieux chat noir, parfaitement laid, mais plein d'esprit et de discretion. Seulement il n'a eu que des gens vulgaires et manque d'usage.*"

Mrs. A.D.T. Whitney, who has written so many helpful stories for girls, is another lover of cats. Cats do not lie curled up on cushions everywhere in her books, as they do in Mrs. Spofford's. But in "Zerub Throop's Experiment" there is an amusing cat story, which, she declares, got so much mixed up with a ghost story that nobody ever knew which was which. And the incident is true in every particular, except the finding of a will or codicil, or something at the end, which is attached for purposes of fiction.

A great deal has been written about the New York *Sun's* famous cats. At my request, Mr. Dana furnished the following description of the interesting *Sun* family. I can only vouch for its veracity by quoting the famous phrase, "If you see it in the *Sun*, it is so."

"Sun office cat (Felis Domestica; var. Journalistica). This is a variation of the common domestic cat, of which but one family is known to science. The habitat of the species is in Newspaper Row; its lair is in the *Sun* building, its habits are nocturnal, and it feeds on discarded copy and anything else of a pseudo-literary nature upon which it can pounce. In dull times it can subsist upon a meagre diet of telegraphic brevities, police court paragraphs, and city jottings; but when the universe is agog with news, it will exhibit the insatiable appetite which is its chief distinguishing mark of difference from the common *felis domestica*. A single member of this family has been known, on a 'rush' night, to devour three and a half columns of presidential possibilities, seven columns of general politics, pretty much all but the head of a large and able-bodied railroad accident, and a full page of miscellaneous news, and then claw the nether garments of the managing editor, and call attention to an appetite still in good working order.

"The progenitrix of the family arrived in the *Sun* office many years ago, and installed herself in a comfortable corner, and within a few short months she had noticeably raised the literary tone of the paper, as well as a large and vociferous family of kittens. These kittens were weaned on reports from country correspondents, and the sight of the six children and the mother cat sitting in a semicircle was one which attracted visitors from all parts of the nation. Just before her death--immediately before, in fact--the mother cat developed a literary taste of her own and drank the contents of an ink-bottle. She was buried with literary honors, and one of her progeny was advanced to the duties and honors of office cat. From this time the line came down, each cat taking the 'laurel greener from the brows of him that uttered nothing base,' upon the death of his predecessor. There is but one blot upon the escutcheon of the family, put there by a recent incumbent who developed a mania at once cannibalistic and infanticidal, and set about making a free lunch of her offspring, in direct violation of the Raines law and the maternal instinct. She died of an overdose of chloroform, and her place was taken by one of the rescued kittens.

"It is the son of this kitten who is the present proud incumbent of the office. Grown to cat-hood, he is a creditable specimen of his family, with beryl eyes, beautiful striped fur, showing fine mottlings of mucilage and ink, a graceful and aspiring tail, an appetite for copy unsurpassed in the annals of his race, and a power and perseverance in vocality, chiefly exercised in the small hours of the morning, that, together with the appetite referred to, have earned for him the name of the Mutilator. The picture herewith given was taken when the animal was a year and a half old. Up to the age of one year the Mutilator made its lair in the inside office with the Snake Editor, until a tragic ending came to their friendship. During a fortnight's absence of the office cat upon important business, the Snake Editor cultivated the friendship of three cockroaches, whom he debauched by teaching them to drink beer spilled upon his desk for that purpose. On the night of the cat's return, the three bugs had become disgracefully intoxicated, and were reeling around the desk beating time with their legs to a rollicking catch sung by the Snake Editor. Before the muddled insects could crawl into a crack, the Mutilator was upon them, and had bolted every one. Then with a look of reproach at the Snake Editor, he drew three perpendicular red lines across that gentleman's features with his claws and departed in high scorn, nor could he ever thereafter be lured into the inner office where the serpent-sharp was laying for him with a space measure. Since that time he has lived in the room occupied by the reporters and news editors.

"Many hundreds of stories, some of them slanderous have been told about the various *Sun* office cats, but we have admitted here none of these false tales. The short sketch given here is beyond suspicion in all its details, as can be vouched for by many men of high position who ought to know better."

CHAPTER IV
CONCERNING STILL OTHER PEOPLE'S CATS

The nearest approach to the real French Salon in America is said to be found in Mrs. Louise Chandler Moulton's Boston drawing-room. In former days, at her weekly Fridays, Sir Richard Coeur de Lion was always present, sitting on the square piano amidst a lot of other celebrities. The autographed photographs of Paderewski, John Drew, and distinguished litterateurs, however, used to lose nothing from the proximity of Mrs. Moulton's favorite maltese friend, who was on the most intimate terms with her for twelve years, and hobnobbed familiarly with most of the lions of one sort or another who have visited Boston and who invariably find their way into this room. If there were flowers on the piano, Richard's nose hovered near them in a perfect abandon of delight. Indeed, his fondness for flowers was a source of constant contention between him and his mistress, who feared lest he knock the souvenirs of foreign countries to the floor in his eagerness to climb wherever flowers were put. He was as dainty about his eating as in his taste for the beautiful, scorning beef and mutton as fit only for coarser mortals, and choosing, like any *gourmet*, to eat only the breast of chicken, or certain portions of fish or lobster. He was not proof against the flavor of liver, at any time; but recognized in it his one weakness,--as the delicate lady may who takes snuff or chews gum on the sly. When Mrs. Moulton first had him, she had also a little dog, and the two, as usual when a kitten is brought up with a dog, became the greatest of friends.

That Richard was a close observer was proved by the way he used to wag his tail, in the same fashion and apparently for the same reasons as the dog. This went on for several years, but when the dog died, the fashion of wagging tails went out, so far as Richard Coeur de Lion was concerned.

He had a fashion of getting up on mantels, the tops of bookcases, or on shelves; and his mistress, fearing demolition of her household Lares and Penates, insisted on his getting down, whereupon Richard would look reproachfully at her, apparently resenting this treatment for days afterward, refusing to come near her and edging off if she tried to make up with him.

When Richard was getting old, a black cat came to Mrs. Moulton, who kept him "for luck," and named him the Black Prince. The older cat was always jealous of the newcomer, and treated him with lofty scorn. When he caught Mrs. Moulton petting the Black Prince, who is a very affectionate fellow Richard fiercely resented it and sometimes refused to have anything to do with her for days afterward, but finally came around and made up in shamefaced fashion.

Mrs. Moulton goes to London usually in the summer, leaving the cats in the care of a faithful maid whom she has had for years. After she sailed, Richard used to come to her door for several mornings, and not being let in as usual, understood that his beloved mistress had left him again, whereupon he kept up a prolonged wailing for some time. He was correspondingly glad to see her on her return in October.

Mrs. Moulton tells the following remarkable cat story:--

"My mother had a cat that lived to be twenty-five years old. He was faithful and fond, and a great pet in the family, of course. About two years before his death, a new kitten was added to the family. This kitten, named Jim, immediately conceived the greatest affection for old Jack, and as the old fellow's senses of sight and smell failed so that he could not go hunting himself, Jim used to do it for both. Every day he brought Jack mice and squirrels and other game as long as he lived. Then, too, he used to wash Jack, lapping him all over as a mother cat does her kitten. He did this, too, as long as he lived. The feebler old Jack grew the more Jim did for him, and when Jack finally died of old age, Jim was inconsolable."

Twenty-five years might certainly be termed a ripe old age for a cat, their average life extending only to ten or twelve years. But I have heard of one who seems to have attained even greater age. The mother of Jane Andrews, the writer on educational and juvenile subjects, had one who lived with them twenty-four years. He had peculiar markings and certain ways of his own about the house quite different from other cats. He disappeared one day when he was twenty-four, and was mourned as dead. But one day, some six or seven years later, an old cat came to their door and asked to be let in. He had the same markings, and on being let in, went directly to his favorite sleeping-places and lay down. He seemed perfectly familiar with the whole place, and went on with his life from that time, just as though he had never been away, showing all his old peculiarities. When he finally died, he must have been thirty-three years old.

Although in other days a great many noted men have been devoted to cats, I do not find that our men of letters to-day know so much about cats. Mr. William Dean Howells says: "I never had a cat, pet or otherwise. I like them, but know nothing of them." Judge Robert Grant says, "My feelings toward cats are kindly and considerate, but not ardent."

Thomas Bailey Aldrich says, "The only cat I ever had any experience with was the one I translated from the French of Emile de La Bedollierre many years ago for the entertainment of my children."[1] Brander Matthews loves them not. George W. Cable answers, when asked if he loves the "harmless, necessary cat," by the Yankee method, and says, "If you had three or four acres of beautiful woods in which were little red squirrels and chipmunks and fifty or more kinds of nesting birds, and every abutting neighbor kept a cat, and none of them kept their cat out of those woods--would you like cats?" which is, indeed, something of a poser.

Colonel Thomas W. Higginson, however, confesses to a great fondness for cats, although he has had no remarkable cats of his own. He tells a story told him by an old sailor at Pigeon Cove, Mass., of a cat which he, the sailor, tried in vain to get rid of. After trying several methods he finally put the cat in a bag, walked a mile to Lane's Cove, tied the cat to a big stone with a firm sailor's knot, took it out in a dory some distance from the shore, and dropped the cat overboard. Then he went back home to find the cat purring on the doorstep.

Those who are familiar with Charles Dudley Warner's "My Summer in a Garden" will not need to be reminded of Calvin and his interesting traits. Mr. Warner says: "I never had but one cat, and he was rather a friend and companion than a cat. When he departed this life I did not care to do as many men do when their partners die, take a 'second.'" The sketch of him in that delightful book is vouched for as correct.

Mr. Edmund Clarence Stedman, too, is a genuine admirer of cats and evidently

---

1   "Mother Michel's Cat."

knows how to appreciate them at their true value. At his home near New York, he and Mrs. Stedman have one who rejoices in the name "Babylon," having originated in Babylon, Long Island. He is a fine large maltese, and attracted a great deal of attention at the New York Cat Show in 1895. "We look upon him as an important member of our family," says Mrs. Stedman, "and think he knows as much as any of us. He despises our two other cats, but he is very fond of human beings and makes friends readily with strangers. He is always present at the family dinner table at meal-time and expects to have his share handed to him carefully. He has a favorite corner in the study and has superintended a great deal of literary work." Mrs. Stedman's long-haired, blue Kelpie took a prize in the show of '95.

Gail Hamilton was naturally a lover of cats, although in her crowded life there was not much time to devote to them. In the last year of her noble life she wrote to a friend as follows: "My two hands were eager to lighten the burden-bearing of a burdened world--but the brush fell from my hand. Now I can only sit in a nook of November sunshine, playing with two little black and white kittens. Well, I never before had time to play with kittens as much as I wished, and when I come outdoors and see them bounding toward me in long, light leaps, I am glad that they leap toward me and not away from me, little soft, fierce sparks of infinite energy holding a mystery of their own as inscrutable as life. And I remember that with all our high art, the common daily sun searches a man for one revealing moment, and makes a truer portrait than the most laborious painter. The divine face of our Saviour, reflected in the pure and noble traits of humanity, will not fail from the earth because my hand has failed in cunning."

One would expect a poet of Ella Wheeler Wilcox's temperament to be passionately fond of cats, just as she is. One would expect, too, that only the most beautiful and luxurious of Persians and Angoras would satisfy her demand for a pet. This is also justifiable, as she has several magnificent cats, about whom she has published a number of interesting stories. Her Madame Ref is quite a noted cat, but Mrs. Wilcox's favorite and the handsomest of all is named Banjo, a gorgeous chinchilla and white Angora, with a silken coat that almost touches the floor and a ruff, or "lord mayor's chain," that is a finger wide. His father was Ajax, his mother was Madame Ref, and Mrs. Wilcox raised him. She has taught him many cunning tricks. He will sit up like a bear, and when his mistress says, "Hug me, Banjo," he puts both white paws around her neck and hugs her tight. Then she says, "Turn the other cheek," and he turns his furry chops for her to kiss. He also plays "dead," and rolls over at command. He, too, is fond of literary work, and superintends his mistress's writing from a drawer of her desk. Goody Two-eyes is another of Mrs. Wilcox's pets, and has one blue and one topaz eye.

Who has not read Agnes Repplier's fascinating essays on "Agrippina" and "A Kitten"? I cannot quite believe she gives cats credit for the capacity for affection which they really possess, but her description of "Agrippina" is charming:--

"Agrippina's beautifully ringed tail flapping across my copy distracts my attention and imperils the neatness of my penmanship. Even when she is disposed to be affable, turns the light of her countenance upon me, watches with attentive curiosity every stroke I make, and softly, with curved paw, pats my pen as it travels over the paper, even in these halcyon moments, though my self-love is flattered by her condescension, I am aware that I should work better and more rapidly if I denied myself this charming companionship. But, in truth, it is impossible for a lover of cats to banish these alert, gentle, and discriminating little friends, who give us just enough of their regard and complaisance to make us hunger for more. M. Fee, the naturalist, who has written so admirably about animals, and who understands, as only a Frenchman can understand, the delicate and subtle organization of a cat, frankly admits that the keynote of its character is independence. It dwells under our roofs, sleeps by our fire, endures our blandishments, and apparently enjoys our society, without for one moment forfeiting its sense of absolute freedom, without acknowledging any servile relation to the human creature who shelters it.

"Rude and masterful souls resent this fine self-sufficiency in a domestic animal, and require that it shall have no will but theirs, no pleasure that does not emanate from them.

"Yet there are people, less magisterial, perhaps, or less exacting, who believe that true friendship, even with an animal, may be built up on mutual esteem and independence; that to demand gratitude is to be unworthy of it; and that obedience is not essential to agreeable and healthy intercourse. A man who owns a dog is, in every sense of the word, its master: the term expresses accurately their mutual relations. But it is ridiculous when applied to the limited possession of a cat. I am certainly not Agrippina's mistress, and the assumption of authority on my part would be a mere empty dignity, like those swelling titles which afford such innocent delight to the Freemasons of our severe republic.

"How many times have I rested tired eyes on her graceful little body, curled up in a ball and wrapped round with her tail like a parcel; or stretched out luxuriously on my bed, one paw coyly covering her face, the other curved gently inwards, as though clasping an invisible treasure. Asleep or awake, in rest or in motion, grave or gay, Agrippina is always beautiful; and it is better to be beautiful than to fetch and carry from the rising to the setting of the sun.

"But when Agrippina has breakfasted and washed, and sits in the sunlight blinking at me with affectionate contempt, I feel soothed by her absolute and unqualified enjoyment. I know how full my day will be of things that I don't want particularly to do, and that are not particularly worth doing; but for her, time and the world hold only this brief moment of contentment. Slowly the eyes close, gently the little body is relaxed. Oh, you who strive to relieve your overwrought nerves and cultivate power through repose, watch the exquisite languor of a drowsy cat, and despair of imitating such perfect and restful grace. There is a gradual yielding of every muscle to the soft persuasiveness of slumber: the flexible frame is curved into tender lines, the head nestles lower, the paws are tucked out of sight: no convulsive throb or start betrays a rebellious alertness: only a faint quiver of unconscious satisfaction, a faint heaving of the tawny sides, a faint gleam of the half-shut yellow eyes, and Agrippina is asleep. I look at her for one wistful moment and then turn resolutely to my work. It were ignoble to wish myself in her place: and yet how charming to be able to settle down to a nap, ***sans peur et sans reproche***, at ten o'clock in the morning."

And again: "When I am told that Agrippina is disobedient, ungrateful, coldhearted, perverse, stupid, treacherous, and cruel, I no longer strive to check the torrent of abuse. I know that Buffon said all this, and much more, about cats, and that people have gone on repeating it ever since, principally because these spirited little beasts have remained just what it pleased Providence to make them, have preserved their primitive freedom through centuries of effete and demoralizing civilization. Why, I wonder, should a great many good men and women cherish an unreasonable grudge against one animal because it does not chance to possess the precise qualities of another? 'My dog fetches my slippers for me every night,' said a friend, triumphantly, not long ago. 'He puts them first to warm by the fire, and then brings them over to my chair, wagging his tail, and as proud as Punch. Would your cat do as much for you, I'd like to know?' Assuredly not. If I waited for Agrippina to fetch me shoes or slippers, I should have no other resource save to join as speedily as possible one of the barefooted religious orders of Italy. But after all, fetching slippers is not the whole duty of domestic pets.

"As for curiosity, that vice which the Abbe Galiani held to be unknown to animals, but which the more astute Voltaire detected in every little dog that he saw peering out of the window of its master's coach, it is the ruling passion of the feline breast. A closet door left ajar, a box with half-closed lid, an open bureau drawer,-- these are the objects that fill a cat with the liveliest interest and delight. Agrippina watches breathlessly the unfastening of a parcel, and tries to hasten matters by clutching actively at the string. When its contents are shown to her, she examines them gravely, and then, with a sigh of relief, settles down to repose. The slightest noise disturbs and irritates her until she discovers its cause. If she hears a footstep in the hall, she runs out to see whose it is, and, like certain troublesome little people I have known, she dearly loves to go to the front door every time the bell is rung. From my window she surveys the street with tranquil scrutiny, and if the boys are playing below, she follows their games with a steady, scornful stare, very different from the wistful eagerness of a friendly dog, quivering to join in the sport. Sometimes the boys catch sight of her, and shout up rudely at her window; and I can never sufficiently admire Agrippina's conduct upon these trying occasions, the well-bred composure with which she affects neither to see nor to hear them, nor to be aware that there are such objectionable creatures as children in the world. Sometimes, too, the terrier that lives next door comes out to sun himself in the street, and, beholding my cat sitting well out of reach, he dances madly up and down the pavement, barking with all his might, and rearing himself on his short legs, in a futile attempt to dislodge her. Then the spirit of evil enters Agrippina's little heart. The window is open and she creeps to the extreme edge of the stone sill, stretches herself at full length, peers down smilingly at the frenzied dog, dangles one paw enticingly in the air, and exerts herself with quiet malice to drive him to desperation. Her sense of humor is awakened by his frantic efforts and by her own absolute security; and not until he is spent with exertion, and lies panting and exhausted on the bricks, does she arch her graceful back, stretch her limbs lazily in the sun, and with one light bound spring from the window to my desk."

And what more delightful word did ever Miss Repplier write than her description of a kitten? It, she says, "is the most irresistible comedian in the world. Its wide-open eyes gleam with wonder and mirth. It darts madly at nothing at all, and then, as though suddenly checked in the pursuit, prances sideways on its hind legs with ridiculous agility and zeal. It makes a vast pretence of climbing the rounds of a chair, and swings by the curtains like an acrobat. It scrambles up a table leg, and is seized with comic horror at finding itself full two feet from the floor. If you hasten to its rescue, it clutches you nervously, its little heart thumping against its furry sides, while its soft paws expand and contract with agitation and relief:--

"'And all their harmless claws disclose,
Like prickles of an early rose.'

"Yet the instant it is back on the carpet it feigns to be suspicious of your interference, peers at you out of 'the tail o' its e'e,' and scampers for protection under the sofa, from which asylum it presently emerges with cautious, trailing steps as though encompassed by fearful dangers and alarms."

Nobody can sympathize with her in the following description better than I, who for years was compelled by the insistence of my Pretty Lady to aid in the bringing up of infants:--

"I own that when Agrippina brought her first-born son--aged two days--and established him in my bedroom closet, the plan struck me at the start as inconvenient. I had prepared another nursery for the little Claudius Nero, and I endeavored for a while to convince his mother that my arrangements were best. But Agrippina was inflexible. The closet suited her in every respect; and, with charming and irresistible flattery, she gave me to understand, in the mute language I knew so well, that she wished her baby boy to be under my immediate protection.

"'I bring him to you because I trust you,' she said as plainly as looks can speak. 'Downstairs they handle him all the time, and it is not good for kittens to be handled. Here he is safe from harm, and here he shall remain,' After a few weak remonstrances, the futility of which I too clearly understood, her persistence carried the day. I removed my clothing from the closet, spread a shawl upon the floor, had the door taken from its hinges, and resigned myself, for the first time in my life, to the daily and hourly companionship of an infant.

"I was amply rewarded. People who require the household cat to rear her off-spring in some remote attic or dark corner of the cellar have no idea of all the diversion and pleasure that they lose. It is delightful to watch the little, blind, sprawling, feeble, helpless things develop swiftly into the grace and agility of kittenhood. It is delightful to see the mingled pride and anxiety of the mother, whose parental love increases with every hour of care, and who exhibits her young family as if they were infant Gracchi, the hope of all their race. During Nero's extreme youth, there were times when Agrippina wearied both of his companionship and of her own maternal duties. Once or twice she abandoned him at night for the greater luxury of my bed, where she slept tranquilly by my side, unmindful of the little wailing cries with which Nero lamented her desertion. Once or twice the heat of early summer tempted her to spend the evening on the porch roof which lay beneath my windows, and I have passed some anxious hours awaiting her return, and wondering what would happen if she never came back, and I were left to bring up the baby by hand.

"But as the days sped on, and Nero grew rapidly in beauty and intelligence, Agrippina's affection for him knew no bounds. She could hardly bear to leave him even for a little while, and always came hurrying back to him with a loud, frightened mew, as if fearing he might have been stolen in her absence. At night she purred over him for hours, or made little gurgling noises expressive of ineffable content. She resented the careless curiosity of strangers, and was a trifle supercilious when the cook stole softly in to give vent to her fervent admiration. But from first to last she shared with me her pride and pleasure; and the joy in her beautiful eyes, as she raised them to mine, was frankly confiding and sympathetic. When the infant Claudius rolled for the first time over the ledge of the closet and lay sprawling on the bedroom floor, it would have been hard to say which of us was the more elated at his prowess."

What became of these most interesting cats, is only hinted at; Miss Repplier's sincere grief at their loss is evident in the following:--

"Every night they retired at the same time and slept upon the same cushion, curled up inextricably into one soft, furry ball. Many times I have knelt by their chair to bid them both good night; and always when I did so, Agrippina would lift her charming head, purr drowsily for a few seconds, and then nestle closer still to her first-born, with sighs of supreme satisfaction. The zenith of her life had been reached. Her cup of contentment was full.

"It is a rude world, even for little cats, and evil chances lie in wait for the petted creatures we strive to shield from harm. Remembering the pangs of separation, the possibilities of unkindness or neglect, the troubles that hide in ambush on every unturned page, I am sometimes glad that the same cruel and selfish blow struck both mother and son, and that they lie together, safe from hurt or hazard, sleeping tranquilly and always, under the shadow of the friendly pines."

Probably no modern cat has been more written about than Miss Mary L. Booth's Muff. There was a "Tippet," but he was early lost. Miss Booth, as the editor of **Harper's Bazar**, was the centre of a large circle of literary and musical people. Her Saturday evenings were to New York what Mrs. Moulton's Fridays are to Boston, the nearest approach to the French salon possible in America. At these Saturday evenings Muff always figured prominently, being dressed in a real lace collar (brought him from Yucatan by Madame la Plongeon, and elaborate and expensive enough for the most fastidious lady), and apparently enjoying the company of noted intellectual people as well as the best of them. And who knows, if he had spoken, what light he might have shed on what seemed to mere mortals as mysterious, abstruse, and occult problems? Perhaps, after all, he liked that "salon" because in reality he found so much to amuse him in the conversation; and perhaps he was, under that guise of friendly interest in noted scientists, reformers, poets, musicians, and litterateurs, only whispering to himself, "O Lord, what fools these mortals be!"

"For when I play with my cat," says Montaigne, "how do I know whether she does not make a jest of me?"

But Muff was a real nobleman among cats, and extraordinarily handsome. He was a great soft gray maltese with white paws and breast--mild, amiable, and uncommonly intelligent. He felt it his duty to help entertain Miss Booth's guests, always; and he more than once, at the beginning of a reception, came into the drawing-room with a mouse in his mouth as his offering to the occasion. Naturally enough "he caused the stampede," as Mrs. Spofford puts it, "that Mr. Gilbert forgot to put into 'Princess Ida' when her Amazons wild demonstrate their courage."

As one of Miss Booth's intimate friends, Mrs. Spofford was much at her house and became early a devoted admirer of Muff's.

"His latter days," she says, "were rendered miserable by a little silky, gray creature, an Angora named Vashti, who was a spark of the fire of the lower regions wrapped round in long silky fur, and who never let him alone one moment: who was full of tail-lashings and racings and leapings and fury, and of the most demonstrative love for her mistress. Once I made them collars with breastplates of tiny dangling bells, nine or ten; it excited them nearly to madness, and they flew up and down stairs like unchained lightning till the trinkets were taken off."

In a house full of birds Muff never touched one, although he was an excellent mouser (who says cats have no conscience?). He was, although so socially inclined toward his mistress's guests, a timid person, and the wild back-yard cats filled him with terror.

"But as one must see something of the world," continues Mrs. Spofford, "he used to jump from lintel to lintel of the windows of the block, if by chance his own were left open, and return when he pleased."

Muff died soon after the death of Miss Booth. Vashti, who was very much admired by all her mistress's literary friends, was given to Miss Juliet Corson.

Miss Edna Dean Proctor, the poet, is another admirer of fine cats. Her favorite, however, was the friend of her childhood called Beauty.

"Beauty was my grandmother's cat," says Miss Proctor, "and the delight of my childhood. To this far-off day I remember her as distinctly as I do my aunt and cousins of that household, and even my dear grandmother herself. I know nothing of her ancestry and am not at all sure that she was royally bred, for she came, one chill night, a little wanderer to the door. But a shred of blue ribbon was clinging to her neck, and she was so pretty, and silky, and winsome that we children at once called her Beauty, and fancied she had strayed from some elegant home where she had been the pet of the household, lapping her milk from finest china and sleeping on a cushion of down. When we had warmed, and fed, and caressed her, we made her bed in a flannel-lined box among our dolls, and the next morning were up before the sun to see her, fearing her owners would appear and carry her away. But no one arrived to claim her, and she soon became an important member of the family, and grew handsomer, we thought, day by day. Her coat was gray with tiger markings, but paws and throat and nose were snowy white, and in spite of her excursions to barns and cellars her constant care kept them spotless--indeed, she was the very Venus of cats for daintiness and grace of pose and movement. To my grandmother her various attitudes had an undoubted meaning. If in a rainy day Beauty washed her face toward the west, her observant mistress would exclaim: 'See, kitty is washing her face to the west. It will clear.' Or, even when the sky was blue, if Beauty turned eastward for her toilet, the comment would be: 'Kitty is washing her face to the east. The wind must be getting "out" (from the sea), and a storm brewing.' And when in the dusk of autumn or winter evenings Beauty ran about the room, chasing her tail or frolicking with her kittens instead of sleeping quietly by the fire as was her wont, my grandmother would look up and say: 'Kitty is wild to-night. The wind will blow hard before morning.' If I sometimes asked how she knew these things, the reply would be, 'My mother told me when I was a little girl.' Now her mother, my great-grandmother, was a distinguished personage in my eyes, having been the daughter of Captain Jonathan Prescott who commanded a company under Sir William Pepperell at the siege of Louisburg and lost his life there; and I could not question the wisdom of colonial times. Indeed, to this hour I have a lingering belief that cats can foretell the weather.

"And what a mouser she was! Before her time we often heard the rats and mice in the walls, but with her presence not one dared to peep, and cupboard and pantry were unmolested. Now and then she carried her forays to hedge and orchard, and I remember one sad summer twilight that saw her bring in a slender brown bird which my grandmother said was the cuckoo we had delighted to hear in the still mornings among the alders by the river. She was scolded and had no milk that night, and we never knew her to catch a bird again.

"O to see her with her kittens! She always hid them in the haymows, and hunting and finding them brought us no end of excitement and pleasure. Twice a day, at least, she would come to the house to be fed, and then how we watched her returning steps, stealing cautiously along the path and waiting behind stack or door the better to observe her--for pussy knew perfectly well that we were eager to see her darlings, and enjoyed misleading and piquing us, we imagined, by taking devious ways. How well I recall that summer afternoon when, soft-footed and alone, I followed her to the floor of the barn. Just as she was about to spring to the mow she espied me, and, turning back, cunningly settled herself as if for a quiet nap in the sunny open door. Determined not to lose sight of her, I threw myself upon the fragrant hay; but in the stillness, the faint sighing of the wind, the far-off ripple of the river, the hazy outline of the hills, the wheeling swallows overhead, were blended at length in an indistinct dream, and I slept, oblivious of all. When I woke, pussy had disappeared, the sun was setting, the cows were coming from the pastures, and I could only return to the house discomfited. That particular family of kittens we never saw till a fortnight later, when the proud mother brought them in one by one, and laid them at my grandmother's feet.

"What became of Beauty is as mysterious as the fate of the Dauphin. To our grief, she disappeared one November day, and we never saw her more. Sometimes we fancied she had been carried off by an admiring traveller: at others we tortured ourselves with the belief that the traditional wildcat of the north woods had devoured her. All we knew was that she had vanished; but when memory pictures that pleasant country home and the dear circle there, white-throated Beauty is always sleeping by the fire."

Miss Fidelia Bridges, the artist, is another devoted cat lover, and at her home at Canaan, Ct., has had several interesting specimens.

"Among my many generations of pet cats," says Miss Bridges, "one aristocratic maltese lady stands out in prominence before all the rest. She was a cat of great personal beauty and independence of character--a remarkable huntress, bringing in game almost as large as herself, holding her beautiful head aloft to keep the great wings of pigeons from trailing on the ground. She and her mother were fast friends from birth to death. When the young maltese had her first brood of kittens, her mother had also a family in another barrel in the cellar. When we went to see the just-arrived family, we found our Lady Malty's bed empty, and there in her mother's barrel were both families and both mothers. A delightful arrangement for the young mother, who could leave her children in the grandmother's care and enjoy her liberty when it pleased her to roam abroad. The young lady had an indomitable will, and when she decided to do a thing nothing would turn her aside. She found a favorite resting-place on a pile of blankets in a dark attic room. This being disapproved of by the elders, the door was kept carefully closed. She then found entrance through a stove-pipe hole, high up on the wall of an adjoining room. A cover was hung over the hole. She sprang up and knocked it off. Then, as a last resort, the hole was papered over like the wall-paper of the room. She looked, made a leap, and crashed through the paper with as merry an air as a circus-rider through his papered hoop. She had a habit of manoeuvring to be shut out of doors at bed-time, and then, when all was still, climbing up to my window by means of a porch over a door beneath it, to pass the night on my bed. In some alterations of the house, the porch was taken away. She looked with dismay for a moment at the destruction of her ladder, then calmly ran up the side of the house to my window, which she always after continued to do.

"Next in importance, perhaps, is my present intimate companion, now ten years old and absolutely deaf, so that we communicate with signs. If I want to attract his attention I step on the floor: if to go to his dinner, I show him a certain blue plate: to call him in at night, I take a lantern outside the door, and the flash of light attracts his attention from a great distance. On one occasion he lived nine months alone in the house while I made a trip to Europe, absolutely refusing all the neighbors' invitations to enter any other house. A friend's gardener brought him his daily rations. As warm weather came, he spent his days in the fields, returning in the night for his food, so that at my return it was two or three days before he discovered that the house was open. The third evening he entered the open door, looked wildly about for a moment, but when I put my hand on him suddenly recognized me and overwhelmed me with affectionate caresses, and for two days and nights would not allow me out of his sight, unable to eat or sleep unless I was close at hand, and following me from room to room and chair to chair. And people say that cats have no affection!"

At the Quincy House in Boston may be seen in the office an oil painting of an immense yellow cat. The first time I noticed the picture, I was proceeding into the dining room, and while waiting for dinner, was amused at seeing the original of the picture walk sedately in, all alone, and going to an empty table, seat himself with majestic grace in a chair. The waiter, seeing him, came forward and pushed up the chair as he would do for any other guest. The cat then waited patiently without putting his paws on the table, or violating any other law of table etiquette, until a plate of meat came, cut up to suit his taste (I did not hear him give his order), and then, placing his front paws on the edge of the table, he ate from his plate. When he had finished, he descended from his table and stalked out of the room with much dignity. He was always regular at his meals, and although he picked out a good seat, did not always sit at the same table. He was in appearance something like the famous orange cats of Venice, and attracted much attention, as might be expected, up to his death, at a ripe old age.

Miss Frances Willard was a cat-lover, too, and had a beautiful cat which is known to all her friends.

"Tootsie" went to Rest Cottage, the home of Frances Willard, when only a kitten, and there he lived, the pet of the household and its guests, until several years ago, when Miss Willard prepared to go abroad. Then she took Tootsie in her arms, carried him to the Drexel kennels in Chicago, and asked their owner, Mrs. Leland Norton, to admit him as a member of her large cat family, where he still lives. To his praise be it spoken, he has never forgotten his old friends at Rest Cottage. To this day, whenever any of them come to call upon him, he honors them with instant and hearty recognition. Miss Willard was sometimes forced to be separated from him more than a year at a time, but neither time nor change had any effect upon Tootsie. At the first sound of her voice he would spring to her side. He is a magnificent Angora, weighing twenty-four pounds, with the long, silky hair, the frill, or lord mayor's chain, the superb curling tail, and the large, full eyes of the thoroughbred. Then he has proved himself of aristocratic tendencies, has beautiful manners, is endowed with the human qualities of memory and discrimination, and is aesthetic in his tastes.

Being the privileged character that he is, Tootsie always eats at the table with the family. He has his own chair and bib, and his manners are said to be exquisite.

CHAPTER V
CONCERNING SOME HISTORIC CATS

It is quite common for writers on the cat to say, "The story of Theophile Gautier's cats is too familiar to need comment." On the contrary, I do not believe it is familiar to the average reader, and that only those who know Gautier's "Menagerie In-time" in the original, recall the particulars of his "White and Black Dynasties." For this reason they shall be repeated in these pages. I use Mrs. Cashel-Hoey's translation, partly in a selfish desire to save myself time and labor, but principally because she has preserved so successfully the sympathetic and appreciative spirit of M. Gautier himself.

"Dynasties of cats, as numerous as those of the Egyptian kings, succeeded each other in my dwelling," says he. "One after another they were swept away by accident, by flight, by death. All were loved and regretted: but life is made up of oblivion, and the memory of cats dies out like the memory of men." After making mention of an old gray cat who always took his part against his parents, and used to bite Madame Gautier's legs when she presumed to reprove her son, he passes on at once to the romantic period, and the commemoration of Childebrand.

"This name at once reveals a deep design of flouting Boileau, whom I did not like then, but have since become reconciled to. Has not Nicholas said:--

"'O le plaisant projet d'un poete ignorant   Que de tant de heros va choisir Childebrant!'

"Now I considered Childebrand a very fine name indeed, Merovingian, mediaeval, and Gothic, and vastly preferable to Agamemnon, Achilles, Ulysses, or any Greek name whatsoever. Romanticism was the fashion of my early days: I have no doubt the people of classical times called their cats Hector, Ajax, or Patroclus. Childebrand was a splendid cat of common kind, tawny and striped with black, like the hose of Saltabadil in 'Le Rois' Amuse.' With his large, green, almond-shaped eyes, and his symmetrical stripes, there was something tigerlike about him that pleased me. Childebrand had the honor of figuring in some verses that I wrote to 'flout' Boileau:--

"Puis je te decrirai ce tableau de Rembrandt Que me fait tant plaisir: et mon chat Childebrand,   Sur mes genoux pose selon son habitude,   Levant sur moi la tete avec inquietude, Suivra les mouvements de mon doigt qui dans l'air Esquisse mon recit pour le rendre plus clair.

"Childebrand was brought in there to make a good rhyme for Rembrandt, the piece being a kind of confession of the romantic faith made to a friend, who was then as enthusiastic as myself about Victor Hugo, Sainte Beuve, and Alfred de Musset.... I come next to Madame Theophile, a 'red' cat, with a white breast, a pink nose, and blue eyes, whom I called by that name because we were on terms of the closest intimacy. She slept at the foot of my bed: she sat on the arm of my chair while I wrote: she came down into the garden and gravely walked about with me: she was present at all my meals, and frequently intercepted a choice morsel on its way from my plate to my mouth. One day a friend who was going away for a short time, brought me his parrot, to be taken care of during his absence. The bird, finding itself in a strange place, climbed up to the top of its perch by the aid of its beak, and rolled its eyes (as yellow as the nails in my arm-chair) in a rather frightened manner, also moving the white membranes that formed its eyelids. Madame Theophile had never seen a parrot, and she regarded the creature with manifest surprise. While remaining as motionless as a cat mummy from Egypt in its swathing bands, she fixed her eyes upon the bird with a look of profound meditation, summoning up all the notions of natural history that she had picked up in the yard, in the garden, and on the roof. The shadow of her thoughts passed over her changing eyes, and we could plainly read in them the conclusion to which her scrutiny led, 'Decidedly this is a green chicken.'

"This result attained, the next proceeding of Madame Theophile was to jump off the table from which she had made her observations, and lay herself flat on the ground in a corner of the room, exactly in the attitude of the panther in Gerome's picture watching the gazelles as they come down to drink at a lake. The parrot followed the movements of the cat with feverish anxiety: it ruffled its feathers, rattled its chain, lifted one of its feet and shook the claws, and rubbed its beak against the edge of its trough. Instinct told it that the cat was an enemy and meant mischief. The cat's eyes were now fixed upon the bird with fascinating intensity, and they said in perfectly intelligible language, which the poor parrot distinctly understood, 'This chicken ought to be good to eat, although it is green.' We watched the scene with great interest, ready to interfere at need. Madame Theophile was creeping nearer and nearer almost imperceptibly; her pink nose quivered, her eyes were half closed, her contractile claws moved in and out of their velvet sheaths, slight thrills of pleasure ran along her backbone at the idea of the meal she was about to make. Such novel and exotic food excited her appetite.

"All in an instant her back took the shape of a bent bow, and with a vigorous and elastic bound she sprang upon the perch. The parrot, seeing its danger, said in a bass voice as grave and deep as M. Prudhomme's own, 'As tu dejeune, Jacquot?'

"This utterance so terrified the cat that she sprang backwards. The blare of a trumpet, the crash and smash of a pile of plates flung to the ground, a pistol shot fired off at her ear, could not have frightened her more thoroughly. All her ornithological ideas were overthrown.

"'Et de quoi? Du roti du roi?' continued the parrot.

"Then might we, the observers, read in the physiognomy of Madame Theophile, 'This is not a bird, it is a gentleman; it talks.'

"'Quand j'ai bu du vin clairet, Tout tourne, tout tourne an cabaret,'

shrieked the parrot in a deafening voice, for it had perceived that its best means of defence was the terror aroused by its speech. The cat cast a glance at me which was full of questioning, but as my response was not satisfactory, she promptly hid herself under the bed, and from that refuge she could not be induced to stir during the whole of the day. People who are not accustomed to live with animals, and who, like Descartes, regard them as mere machines, will think that I lend unauthorized meanings to the acts of the 'volatile' and the 'quadruped,' but I have only faithfully translated their ideas into human language. The next day Madame Theophile plucked up courage and made another attempt, which was similarly repulsed. From that moment she gave it up, accepting the bird as a variety of man.

"This dainty and charming animal was extremely fond of perfumes, especially of patchouli and the scent exhaled by India shawls. She was also very fond of music, and would listen, sitting on a pile of music-books, while the fair singers who came to try the critic's piano filled his room with melody. All the time Madame Theophile would evince great pleasure. She was, however, made nervous by certain notes, and at the high *la* she would tap the singer's mouth with her paw. This was very amusing, and my visitors delighted in making the experiment. It never failed; the dilettante in fun was not to be deceived.

"The rule of the 'White Dynasty' belonged to a later epoch, and was inaugurated in the person of a pretty little kitten as white as a powder puff, who came from Havana. On account of his spotless whiteness he was called Pierrot; but when he grew up this name was very properly magnified into Don-Pierrot-de-Navarre, which was far more majestic, and suggested 'grandee-ism.' [M. Theophile Gautier lays it down as a dogma that all animals with whom one is much taken up, and who are 'spoiled,' become delightfully good and amiable. Don-Pierrot-de-Navarre successfully supported his master's theory; perhaps he suggested it.]

"He shared in the life of the household with the enjoyment of quiet fireside friendship that is characteristic of cats. He had his own place near the fire, and there he would sit with a convincing air of comprehension of all that was talked of and of interest in it; he followed the looks of the speakers, and uttered little sounds toward them as though he, too, had objections to make and opinions to give upon the literary subjects which were most frequently discussed. He was very fond of books, and when he found one open on a table he would lie down on it, turn over the edges of the leaves with his paws, and after a while fall asleep, for all the world as if he had been reading a fashionable novel. He was deeply interested in my writing, too; the moment I took up my pen he would jump upon the desk, and follow the movement of the penholder with the gravest attention, making a little movement with his head at the beginning of each line. Sometimes he would try to take the pen out of my hand.

"Don-Pierrot-de-Navarre never went to bed until I had come in. He would wait for me just inside the outer door and rub himself to my legs, his back in an arch, with a glad and friendly purring. Then he would go on before me, preceding me with a page-like air, and I have no doubt, if I had asked him, he would have carried the candlestick. Having thus conducted me to my bedroom, he would wait quietly while I undressed, and then jump on my bed, take my neck between his paws, gently rub my nose with his own, and lick me with his small, pink tongue, as rough as a file, uttering all the time little inarticulate cries, which expressed as clearly as any words could do his perfect satisfaction at having me with him again. After these caresses he would perch himself on the back of the bedstead and sleep there, carefully balanced, like a bird on a branch. When I awoke, he would come down and lie beside me until I got up.

"Pierrot was as strict as a concierge in his notions of the proper hour for all good people to return to their homes. He did not approve of anything later than midnight. In those days we had a little society among friends, which we called 'The Four Candles,'--the light in our place of meeting being restricted to four candles in silver candlesticks, placed at the four corners of the tables. Sometimes the talk became so animated that I forgot all about time, and twice or three times Pierrot sat up for me until two o'clock in the morning. After a while, however, my conduct in this respect displeased him, and he retired to rest without me. I was touched by this mute protest against my innocent dissipation, and thenceforth came home regularly at twelve o'clock. Nevertheless, Pierrot cherished the memory of my of-fence for some time; he waited to test the reality of my repentance, but when he was convinced that my conversion was sincere, he deigned to restore me to his good graces, and resumed his nocturnal post in the anteroom.

"To gain the friendship of a cat is a difficult thing. The cat is a philosophical, methodical, quiet animal, tenacious of its own habits, fond of order and cleanliness, and it does not lightly confer its friendship. If you are worthy of its affection, a cat will be your friend, but never your slave. He keeps his free will, though he loves, and he will not do for you what he thinks unreasonable; but if he once gives him-self to you, it is with such absolute confidence, such fidelity of affection. He makes himself the companion of your hours of solitude, melancholy, and toil. He remains for whole evenings on your knee, uttering his contented purr, happy to be with you, and forsaking the company of animals of his own species. In vain do melodious mewings on the roof invite him to one of those cat parties in which fish bones play the part of tea and cakes; he is not to be tempted away from you. Put him down and he will jump up again, with a sort of cooing sound that is like a gentle reproach; and sometimes he will sit upon the carpet in front of you, looking at you with eyes so melting, so caressing, and so human, that they almost frighten you, for it is impossible to believe that a soul is not there.

"Don-Pierrot-de-Navarre had a sweetheart of the same race and of as snowy a whiteness as himself. The ermine would have looked yellow by the side of Seraphita, for so this lovely creature was named, in honor of Balzac's Swedenborgian romance. Seraphita was of a dreamy and contemplative disposition. She would sit on a cushion for hours together, quite motionless, not asleep, and following with her eyes, in a rapture of attention, sights invisible to mere mortals. Caresses were agreeable to her, but she returned them in a very reserved manner, and only in the case of persons whom she favored with her rarely accorded esteem. She was fond of luxury, and it was always upon the handsomest easy-chair, or the rug that would best show off her snowy fur, that she would surely be found. She devoted a great deal of time to her toilet, her glossy coat was carefully smoothed every morning. She washed herself with her paw, and licked every atom of her fur with her pink tongue until it shone like new silver. When any one touched her, she instantly effaced all trace of the contact; she could not endure to be tumbled. An idea of aristocracy was suggested by her elegance and distinction, and among her own people she was a duchess at least. She delighted in perfumes, would stick her nose into bouquets, bite scented handkerchiefs with little spasms of pleasure, and walk about among the scent bottles on the toilet table, smelling at their stoppers; no doubt, she would have used the powder puff if she had been permitted. Such was Seraphita, and never did cat more amply justify a poetic name. I must mention here that, in the days of the White Dynasty, I was also the happy possessor of a family of white rats, and that the cats, always supposed to be their natural, invariable, and irreconcilable enemies, lived in perfect harmony with my pet rodents. The rats never showed the slightest distrust of the cats, nor did the cats ever betray their confidence. Don-Pierrot-de-Navarre was very much attached to them. He would sit close to their cage and observe their gambols for hours together, and if by any chance the door of the room in which they were left was shut, he would scratch and mew gently until some one came to open it and allow him to rejoin his little white friends, who would often come out of the cage and sleep close to him. Seraphita, who was of a more reserved and disdainful temper, and who disliked the musky odor of the white rats, took no part in their games; but she never did them any harm, and would let them pass before her without putting out a claw.

"Don-Pierrot-de-Navarre, who came from Havana, required a hothouse temperature: and this he always had in his own apartments. The house was, however, surrounded by extensive gardens, divided by railings, through and over which cats could easily climb, and in those gardens were trees inhabited by a great number of birds. Pierrot would frequently take advantage of an open door to get out of an evening and go a-hunting through the wet grass and flower-beds: and, as his mewing under the windows when he wanted to get in again did not always awaken the sleepers in the house, he frequently had to stay out until morning. His chest was delicate, and one very chilly night he caught a cold which rapidly developed into phthisis. At the end of a year of coughing, poor Don Pierrot had wasted to a skeleton, and his coat, once so silky, was a dull, harsh white. His large, transparent eyes looked unnaturally large in his shrunken face: the pink of his little nose had faded, and he dragged himself slowly along the sunny side of the wall with a melancholy air, looking at the yellow autumnal leaves as they danced and whirled in the wind. Nothing is so touching as a sick animal: it submits to suffering with such gentle and sad resignation. We did all in our power to save Pierrot: a skilful doctor came to see him, felt his pulse, sounded his lungs, and ordered him ass's milk. He drank the prescribed beverage very readily out of his own especial china saucer. For hours together he lay stretched upon my knee, like the shadow of a sphinx. I felt his spine under my finger tips like the beads of a rosary, and he tried to respond to my caresses by a feeble purr that resembled a death-rattle. On the day of his death he was lying on his side panting, and suddenly, with a supreme effort, he rose and came to me. His large eyes were opened wide, and he gazed at me with a look of intense supplication, a look that seemed to say, 'Save me, save me, you, who are a man.' Then he made a few faltering steps, his eyes became glassy, and he fell down, uttering so lamentable a cry, so dreadful and full of anguish, that I was struck dumb and motionless with horror. He was buried at the bottom of the garden under a white rose tree, which still marks the place of his sepulture. Three years later Seraphita died, and was buried by the side of Don Pierrot. With her the White Dynasty became extinct, but not the family. This snow-white couple had three children, who were as black as ink. Let any one explain that mystery who can. The kittens were born in the early days of the great renown of Victor Hugo's 'Les Miserables,' when everybody was talking of the new masterpiece, and the names of the personages in it were in every mouth. The two little male creatures were called Enjolras and Gavroche, and their sister received the name of Eponine. They were very pretty, and I trained them to run after a little ball of paper and bring it back to me when I threw it into the corner of the room. In time they would follow the ball up to the top of the bookcase, or fish for it behind boxes or in the bottom of china vases with their dainty little paws. As they grew up they came to disdain those frivolous amusements, and assumed the philosophical and meditative quiet which is the true temperament of the cat.

"To the eyes of the careless and indifferent observer, three black cats are just three black cats, but those who are really acquainted with animals know that their physiognomy is as various as that of the human race. I was perfectly well able to distinguish between these little faces, as black as Harlequin's mask, and lighted up by disks of emerald with golden gleams. Enjolras, who was much the handsomest of the three, was remarkable for his broad, leonine head and full whiskers, strong shoulders, and a superb feathery tail. There was something theatrical and pretentious in his air, like the posing of a popular actor. His movements were slow, undulatory, and majestic: so circumspect was he about where he set his feet down that he always seemed to be walking among glass and china. His disposition was by no means stoical, and he was much too fond of food to have been approved of by his namesake. The temperate and austere Enjolras would certainly have said to him, as the angel said to Swedenborg, 'You eat too much.' I encouraged his gastronomical tastes, and Enjolras attained a very unusual size and weight.

"Gavroche was a remarkably knowing cat, and looked it. He was wonderfully active, and his twists, twirls, and tumbles were very comic. He was of a Bohemian temperament, and fond of low company. Thus he would occasionally compromise the dignity of his descent from the illustrious Don-Pierrot-de-Navarre, grandee of Spain of the first class, and the Marquesa Dona Seraphita, of aristocratic and disdainful bearing. He would sometimes return from his expeditions to the street, accompanied by gaunt, starved companions, whom he had picked up in his wanderings, and he would stand complacently by while they bolted the contents of his plate of food in a violent hurry and in dread of dispersion by a broomstick or a shower of water. I was sometimes tempted to say to Gavroche, 'A nice lot of friends you pick up,' but I refrained, for, after all, it was an amiable weakness: he might have eaten his dinner all by himself.

"The interesting Eponine was more slender and graceful than her brothers, and she was an extraordinarily sensitive, nervous, and electric animal. She was passionately attached to me, and she would do the honors of my hermitage with perfect grace and propriety. When the bell rang, she hastened to the door, received the visitors, conducted them to the salon, made them take seats, talked to them--yes, talked, with little coos, murmurs, and cries quite unlike the language which cats use among themselves, and which bordered on the articulate speech of man. What did she say? She said quite plainly: 'Don't be impatient: look at the pictures, or talk with me, if I amuse you. My master is coming down.' On my appearing she would retire discreetly to an arm-chair or the corner of the piano, and listen to the conversation without interrupting it, like a well-bred animal accustomed to good society.

"Eponine's intelligence, fine disposition, and sociability led to her being elevated by common consent to the dignity of a person, for reason, superior instinct, plainly governed her conduct. That dignity conferred on her the right to eat at table like a person, and not in a corner on the floor, from a saucer, like an animal. Eponine had a chair by my side at breakfast and dinner, but in consideration of her size she was privileged to place her fore paws on the table. Her place was laid, without a knife and fork, indeed, but with a glass, and she went regularly through dinner, from soup to dessert, awaiting her turn to be helped, and behaving with a quiet propriety which most children might imitate with advantage. At the first stroke of the bell she would appear, and when I came into the dining room she would be at her post, upright in her chair, her fore paws on the edge of the tablecloth, and she would present her smooth forehead to be kissed, like a well-bred little girl who was affectionately polite to relatives and old people. When we had friends to dine with us, Eponine always knew that company was expected. She would look at her place, and if a knife, fork, and spoon lay near her plate she would immediately turn away and seat herself on the piano-stool, her invariable refuge. Let those who deny the possession of reason to animals explain, if they can, this little fact, apparently so simple, but which contains a world of induction. From the presence near her plate of those implements which only man can use, the observant and judicious cat concluded that she ought on this occasion to give way to a guest, and she hastened to do so. She was never mistaken: only, when the visitor was a person whom she knew and liked, she would jump on his knee and coax him for a bit off his plate by her graceful caresses. She survived her brothers, and was my dear companion for several years.... Such is the chronicle of the Black Dynasty."

Although cats have no place in the Bible, neither can their enemies who sing the praise of the dog, find much advantage there: for that most excellent animal is referred to in anything but a complimentary fashion--"For without are dogs and sorcerers."

The great prophet of Allah, however, knew a good cat when he saw it. "Muezza" even contributed her small share to the development of the Mahometan system: for did she not sit curled up in her master's sleeve, and by her soft purring soothe and deepen his meditations? And did she not keep him dreaming so long that she finally became exhausted herself, and fell asleep in his flowing sleeve; whereupon did not Mahomet, rather than disturb her, and feeling that he must be about his Allah's business, cut off his sleeve rather than disturb the much loved Muezza? The nurses of Cairo tell this story to their young charges to this day.

Cardinal Richelieu had many a kitten, too; and morose and ill-tempered as he was, found in them much amusement. His love for them, however, was not that unselfish love which led Mahomet to cut off his sleeve; but simply a selfish desire for passing amusement. He cared nothing for that most interesting process, the development of a kitten into a cat, and the study of its individuality which is known only to the real lover of cats. For it is recorded of him that as soon as his pets were three months old he sent them away, evidently not caring where, and procured new ones.

M. Champfleury, however, thinks it possible that there may not be any real foundation for this story about Richelieu. He refers to the fact that Moncrif says not a word about the celebrated cardinal's passion for those creatures; but he does say, "Everybody knows that one of the greatest ministers France ever possessed, M. Colbert, always had a number of kittens playing about that same cabinet in which so many institutions, both honorable and useful to the nation, had their origin." Can it be that Richelieu has been given credit for Colbert's virtues?

In various parts of Chateaubriand's "Memoires" may be found eulogiums on the cat. So well known was his fondness for them, that even when his other feelings and interests faded with age and decay, his affections for cats remained strong to the end. This love became well known to all his compeers, and once on an embassy to Rome the Pope gave him a cat. He was called "Micetto." According to Chateaubriand's biographer, M. de Marcellus, "Pope Leo XII's cat could not fail to reappear in the description of that domestic hearth where I have so often seen him basking. In fact, Chateaubriand has immortalized his favorite in the sketch which begins, 'My companion is a big cat, of a greyish red.'" This ecclesiastical pet was always dignified and imposing in manners, ever conscious that he had been the gift of a sovereign pontiff, and had a tremendous weight of reputation to maintain. He used to stroke his tail when he desired Madame Recamier to know that he was tired.

"I love in the cat," said Chateaubriand to M. de Marcellus, "that independent and almost ungrateful temper which prevents it from attaching itself to any one: the indifference with which it passes from the salon to the house-top. When you caress it, it stretches itself out and arches its back, indeed: but that is caused by physical pleasure, not, as in the case of the dog, by a silly satisfaction in loving and being faithful to a master who returns thanks in kicks. The cat lives alone, has no need of society, does not obey except when it likes, and pretends to sleep that it may see the more clearly, and scratches everything that it can scratch. Buffon has belied the cat: I am laboring at its rehabilitation, and hope to make of it a tolerably good sort of animal, as times go."

Cardinal Wolsey, Lord High Chancellor of England, was another cat-lover, and his superb cat sat in a cushioned arm-chair by his side in the zenith of his pride and power, the only one in that select circle who was not obliged to don a wig and robe while acting in a judicial capacity. Then there was Bouhaki, the proud Theban cat that used to wear gold earrings as he sat at the feet of King Hana, his owner, perhaps, but not his master, and whose reproduction in the tomb of Hana in the Necropolis at Thebes, between his master's feet in a statue, is one of the most ancient reproductions of a cat. And Sainte-Beuve, whose cat used to roam at will over his desk and sit or lie on the precious manuscripts no other person was allowed to touch; it is flattering to know that the great Frenchman and I have one habit in common; and Miss Repplier owns to it too. "But Sainte-Beuve," says she, "probably had sufficient space reserved for his own comfort and convenience. I have not; and Agrippina's beautifully ringed tail flapping across my copy distracts my attention and imperils the neatness of my penmanship." And even as I write these pages, does the Pretty

Lady's daughter Jane lie on my copy and gaze lovingly at me as I work.

Julian Hawthorne is another writer whose cat is an accompaniment of his working hours. In this connection we must not forget M. Brasseur Wirtgen, a student of natural history who writes of his cat: "My habit of reading," he says, "which divided us from each other in our respective thoughts, prejudiced my cat very strongly against my books. Sometimes her little head would project its profile on the page which I was perusing, as though she were trying to discover what it was that thus absorbed me: doubtless, she did not understand why I should look for my happiness beyond the presence of a devoted heart. Her solicitude was no less manifest when she brought me rats or mice. She acted in this case exactly as if I had been her son: dragging enormous rats, still in the throes of death, to my feet: and she was evidently guided by logic in offering me a prey commensurate with my size, for she never presented any such large game to her kittens. Her affectionate attention invariably caused her a severe disappointment. Having laid the product of her hunting expedition at my feet, she would appear to be greatly hurt by my indifference to such delicious fare."

That Tasso had a cat we know because he wrote a sonnet to her. Alfred de Musset's cats are apostrophized in his verses. Dr. Johnson's Hodge held a soft place for many years in the gruff old scholar's breast. And has not every one heard how the famous Dr. Johnson fetched oysters for his beloved Hodge, lest the servants should object to the trouble, and vent their displeasure on his favorite?

Nor can one forget Sir Isaac Newton and his cats: for is it not alleged that the great man had two holes cut in his barn door, one for the mother, and a smaller one for the kitten?

Byron was fond of cats: in his establishment at Ravenna he had five of them. Daniel Maclise's famous portrait of Harriet Martineau represents that estimable woman sitting in front of a fireplace and turning her face to receive the caress of her pet cat crawling to a resting-place upon her mistress's shoulder.

Although La Fontaine in his fables shows such a delicate appreciation of their character and ways, it is doubtful whether he honestly loved cats. But his friend and patron, the Duchess of Bouillon, was so devoted to them that she requested the poet to make her a copy with his own hand of all his fables in which pussy appears. The exercise-book in which they were written was discovered a few years ago among the Bouillon papers.

Baudelaire, it is said, could never pass a cat in the street without stopping to stroke and fondle it. "Many a time," said Champfleury, "when he and I have been walking together, have we stopped to look at a cat curled luxuriously in a pile of fresh white linen, revelling in the cleanliness of the newly ironed fabrics. Into what fits of contemplation have we fallen before such windows, while the coquettish laundresses struck attitudes at the ironing boards, under the mistaken impression that we were admiring them." It was also related of Baudelaire that, "going for the first time to a house, he is restless and uneasy until he has seen the household cat. But when he sees it, he takes it up, kisses and strokes it, and is so completely absorbed in it, that he makes no answer to what is said to him."

Professor Huxley's notorious fondness for cats was a fad which he shared with Paul de Koch, the novelist, who, at one time, kept as many as thirty cats in his house. Many descriptions of them are to be found scattered through his novels. His chief favorite, Fromentin, lived eleven years with him.

Pierre Loti has written a charming and most touching history of two of his cats--Moumette Blanche and Moumette Chinoise--which all true cat-lovers should make a point of reading.

Algernon Swinburne, the poet, is devoted to cats. His favorite is named Atossa. Robert Southey was an ardent lover of cats. Most people have read his letter to his friend Bedford, announcing the death of one. "Alas, Grosvenor," he wrote, "this day poor Rumpel was found dead, after as long and happy a life as cat could wish for, if cats form wishes on that subject. His full titles were: The Most Noble, the Archduke Rumpelstiltzchen, Marcus Macbum, Earl Tomlefnagne, Baron Raticide, Waowhler and Scratch. There should be a court-mourning in Catland, and if the Dragon (your pet cat) wear a black ribbon round his neck, or a band of crape *a la militaire* round one of his fore paws it will be but a becoming mark of respect." Then the poet-laureate adds, "I believe we are each and all, servants included, more sorry for his loss, or, rather, more affected by it, than any of us would like to confess."

Josh Billings called his favorite cat William, because he considered no shorter name fitted to the dignity of his character. "Poor old man," he remarked one day, to a friend, "he has fits now, so I call him Fitz-William."

CHAPTER VI
CONCERNING CATS IN ENGLAND

I f the growing fancy for cats in this country is benefiting the feline race as a whole, they have to thank the English people for it. For certain cats in England are held at a value that seems preposterous to unsophisticated Americans. At one cat and bird show, held at the Crystal Palace, near London, some of the cats were valued at thirty-five hundred pounds sterling ($17,500)--as much as the price of a first-class race-horse.

For more than a quarter of a century National Cat Shows have been held at Crystal Palace and the Westminster Aquarium, which have given great stimulus to the breeding of fine cats, and "catteries" where high-priced cats and kittens are raised are common throughout the country.

England was the first, too, to care for lost and deserted cats and dogs. At Battersea there is a Temporary Home for both these unfortunates, where between twenty and twenty-five thousand dogs and cats are sheltered and fed. The objects of this home, which is supported entirely by voluntary subscriptions, are to restore lost pets to their owners, to find suitable homes for unclaimed cats and dogs, and to painlessly destroy useless and diseased ones. There is a commodious cat's house where pets may be boarded during their owner's absence; and a separate house where lost and deserted felines are sheltered, fed, and kindly tended.

Since long before Whittington became Lord Mayor of London, indeed, cats have been popular in England: for did not the law protect them? As to the truth of the story of Whittington's cat, there has been much earnest discussion. Although Whittington lived from about 1360 to 1425, the story seems to have been pretty generally accepted for three hundred years after his death. A portrait still exists of him, with one hand holding a cat, and when his old house was remodelled in recent times, a carved stone was found in it showing a boy with a cat in his arms. Several similar tales have been found, it is argued, in which the heroes in different countries have started to make a fortune by selling a cat. But as rats and mice were extremely common then, and it has been shown that a single pair of rats will in three years multiply into over six hundred thousand, which will eat as much as sixty-four thousand men, why shouldn't a cat be deemed a luxury even for a king's palace? The argument that the cat of Whittington was a "cat," or boat used for carrying coal, is disproved by the fact that no account of such vessels in Whittington's time can be found, and also that the trade in coal did not begin in Europe for some time afterward. And there really seems nothing improbable in the story that at a time when a kitten big enough to kill mice brought fourpence in England, such an animal, taken to a rat-infested, catless country, might not be sold for a sum large enough to start an enterprising youth in trade. Surely, the beginnings of some of our own railroad kings and financiers may as well look doubtful to future generations.

It is a pretty story--that of Whittington; how he rose from being a mere scullion at fourteen, to being "thrice Lord Mayor of London." According to what are claimed to be authentic documents, the story is something more than a nursery tale, and runs thus: Poor Dick Whittington was born at Shropshire, of such very poor parents that the boy, being of an ambitious nature, left home at fourteen, and walked to London, where he was taken into the hospital of St. John at Clerkenwell, in a menial capacity. The prior, noticing his good behavior and diligent conduct, took a fancy to him, and obtained him a position in a Mr. Fitzwarren's household on Tower Hill. For some time at this place his prospects did not improve; he was nothing but a scullion, ridiculed and disliked by the cook and other servants. Add to this the fact that an incredible swarm of mice and rats infested the miserable room in which he slept, and it would seem that he was indeed a "poor Richard." One fortunate day, however, he conceived the idea of buying a cat, and as good luck would have it, he was enabled within a few days to earn a penny or two by blacking the boots of a guest at the house. That day he met a woman with a cat for sale, and after some dickering (for she asked more money for it than the boy possessed in the world), Dick Whittington carried home his cat and put it in a cupboard or closet opening from his room. That night when he retired he let the cat out of the cupboard, and she evidently had "no end of fun"; for, according to these authentic accounts, "she destroyed all the vermin which ventured to make their appearance." For some time after that she passed her days in the cupboard (in hiding from the cook) and her nights in catching mice.

And then came the change. Mr. Fitzwarren was fitting out a vessel for Algiers, and kindly offered all his servants a chance to send something to barter with the natives. Poor Dick had nothing but his cat, but the commercial instinct was even then strong within him, and with an enterprise worthy of the early efforts of any of our self-made men, he decided to send that, and accordingly placed it, "while the tears run plentifully down his cheeks," in the hands of the master of the vessel. She must have been a most exemplary cat, for by the time they had reached Algiers, the captain was so fond of her that he allowed no one to handle her but himself. Not even he, however, expected to turn her into money; but the opportunity soon came.

At a state banquet, given by the Dey, the captain and his officers were astonished to notice that rats and mice ran freely in and out, stealing half the choice food, which was spread on the carpet; and this was a common, every-day occurrence. The captain saw his, or Whittington's, opportunity, and stated that he knew a certain remedy for this state of affairs; whereupon he was invited to dinner next day, to which he carried the cat, and the natural consequence ensued. This sudden and swift extermination of the pests drove the Dey and his court half frantic with delight; and the captain, who must have been the original progenitor of the Yankee race, drove a sharp bargain by assuming to be unwilling to part with the cat, so that the Dey finally "sent on board his ship the choicest commodities, consisting of gold, jewels, and silks."

Meanwhile, things had gone from bad to worse with the youth, destined to become not only Lord Mayor of London, but the envy and admiration of future generations of youths; and he made up his mind to run away from his place. This he did, but while he was on his way to more rural scenes, he sat down on a stone at the foot of Highgate Hill (a stone that still remains marked as "Whittington's Stone") and paused to reflect on his prospects. His thoughts turned back to the home he had left, where he had at least plenty to eat, and, although the "authentic reports" use a great many words to tell us so, the boy was homesick. Just then the sound of Bow Bells reached him, and to his youthful fancy seemed to call him back:--

"Return, return, Whittington;   Thrice Lord Mayor of London."

Thus the old tale hath it. At any rate, the boy gave up the idea of flight and went back to Mr. Fitzwarren's house. The second night after, his master sent for him in the midst of one of the cook's tirades, and going to the "parlour" he was apprised of his sudden wealth; because, added to the rest of his good luck, that captain happened to be an honest man. And then he went into trade and married the daughter of Mr. Fitzwarren and became Lord Mayor of London, and lived even happier ever after than they do in most fairy tales. And everybody, even the cook, admired and loved him after he had money and position, as has been known to happen outside of fairy tales.

Whether or not cats in England owe anything of their position to-day to the Whittington story, it is certain that they have more really appreciating friends there than in any other country. The older we grow in the refinements of civilization, the more we value the finely bred cat. In England it has long been the custom to register the pedigree of cats as carefully as dog-fanciers in this country do with their fancy pets. Some account of the Cat Club Stud Book and Register will be found in the next chapter. Queen Victoria, and the Princess of Wales, and indeed many members of the nobility are cat-lovers, and doubtless this fact influences the general sentiment in England.

Among the most devoted of Pussy's English admirers is the Hon. Mrs. McLaren Morrison, who is the happy possessor of some of the most perfect dogs and cats that have graced the bench. She lives at Kepwick Park, in her stately home in Yorkshire--a lovely spot, commanding a delightful view of picturesque Westmoreland on one side and on the other three surrounded and sheltered by hills and moors. Some of her pets go with her, however, to her flat in Queen Anne's Mansions, and even to her residence in Calcutta. It is at Kepwick Park that Mrs. McLaren Morrison has her celebrated "catteries." Here there are magnificent blue, black and silver and red Persians; snowy white, blue-eyed beauties; grandly marked English tabbies; handsome blue Russians, with their gleaming yellow-topaz eyes; some Chinese cats, with their long, edge-shaped heads, bright golden eyes, and shiny, short-haired black fur; and a pair of Japanese pussies, pure white and absolutely without tails. One of the handsomest specimens of the feline race ever seen is her blue Persian, Champion

Monarch, who, as a kitten in 1893, won the gold medal at the Crystal Palace given for the best pair of kittens in the show, and the next year the Beresford Challenge Cup at Cruft's Show, for the best long-haired cat, besides taking many other honors. Among other well-known prize winners are the champions Snowball and Forget-me-not, both pure white, with lovely turquoise-blue eyes. Of Champion Nizam (now dead) that well-known English authority on cats, Mr. A.A. Clark, said his was the grandest head of any cat he had ever seen. Nizam was a perfect specimen of that rare and delicate breed of cats, a pure chinchilla. The numberless kittens sporting all day long are worthy of the art of Madame Henriette Ronner, and one could linger for hours in these delightful and most comfortable catteries watching their gambols. The gentle mistress of this fair and most interesting domain, the Hon. Mrs. McLaren Morrison herself, is one of the most attractive and fascinating women of the day--one who adds to great personal beauty all the charm of mental culture and much travel. She has made Kepwick Park a veritable House Beautiful with the rare curios and art treasures collected with her perfect taste in the many lands she has visited, and it is as interesting and enjoyable to a virtuoso as it is to an animal lover. Mrs. McLaren Morrison exhibits at all the cat shows, often entering as many as twenty-five cats. Other English ladies who exhibit largely are Mrs. Herring, of Lestock House, and Miss Cockburn Dickinson, of Surrey. Mrs. Herring's Champion Jimmy is very well known as a first prize-winner in many shows. He is a short-haired, exquisitely marked silver tabby valued at two thousand pounds ($10,000).

Another feline celebrity also well known to frequenters of English cat shows, is Madame L. Portier's magnificent and colossal Blue Boy, whose first appearance into this world was made on the day sacred to St. Patrick, 1895. He has a fine pedigree, and was raised by Madame Portier herself. Blue Boy commenced his career as a show cat, or rather kitten, at three months old, when he was awarded a first prize, and when the judge told his mistress that if he fulfilled his early promise he would make a grand cat. This he has done, and is now one of the finest specimens of his kind in England. He weighs over seventeen pounds, and always has affixed to his cage on the show-bench this request, "Please do not lift this cat by the neck; he is too heavy." He has long dark blue fur, with a ruff of a lighter shade and brilliant topaz eyes. Already Blue Boy has taken many prizes. He is a gelded cat and one of the fortunate cats who have "Not for Sale" after their names in the show catalogues.

To Mrs. C. Hill's beautiful long-haired Patrick Blue fell the honor, at the Crystal Palace Show in 1896, of a signed and framed photograph of the Prince of Wales, presented by his Royal Highness for the best long-haired cat in the show, irrespective of sex or nationality. Besides the prize given by the Prince, Patrick Blue was the proud winner of the Beresford Challenge Cup for the best blue long-haired cat, and the India Silver Bowl for the best Persian. He also was born on St. Patrick's Day, hence his name. He was bred by Mrs. Blair Maconochie, his father, Blue Ruin I, being a celebrated gold medallist. His mother, Sylvia, who belongs to Mrs. Maconochie, has never been shown, her strong point being her lovely color, which is most happily reproduced in her perfect son. Patrick Blue has all the many charms of a petted cat, and was undoubtedly one of the prominent attractions of the first Championship Show of the National Cat Club in 1896.

Silver Lambkin is another very famous English cat, owned by Miss Gresham, of Surrey. Princess Ranee, owned by Miss Freeland, of Mottisfont, near Romney; Champion Southsea Hector, owned by Miss Sangster, at Southsea; champions Prince Victor and Shelly, of Kingswood (both of whom have taken no end of prizes), are other famous English cats.

Topso, a magnificent silver tabby male, belonging to Miss Anderson Leake, of Dingley Hill, was at one time the best long-haired silver tabby in England, and took the prize on that account in 1887; his sons, daughters, grandsons, and granddaughters, have all taken prizes at Crystal Palace in the silver tabby classes, since that time. Lady Marcus Beresford has for the last fifteen years made quite a business of the breeding and rearing of cats. At Bishopsgate, near Egham, she has what is without doubt the finest cattery. "I have applications from all parts of the world for my cats and kittens," said Lady Marcus, in a talk about her hobby, "and I may tell you that it is largely because of this that I founded the Cat Club, which has for its object the general welfare of the cat and the improvement of the breed. My catteries were established in 1890, and at one time I had as many as 150 cats and kittens. Some of my pets live in a pretty cottage covered with creepers, which might well be called Cat Cottage. No expense has been spared in the fittings of the rooms, and every provision is made for warmth and ventilation. One room is set apart for the girl who takes entire charge of and feeds the pussies. She has a boy who works with her and performs the rougher tasks. There is a small kitchen for cooking the meals for the cats, and this is fitted with every requisite. On the walls are racks to hold the white enamelled bowls and plates used for the food. There is a medicine chest, which contains everything that is needful for prompt and efficacious treatment in case pussy becomes sick. On the wall are a list of the names and a full description of all the inmates of the cattery, and a set of rules to be observed by both the cats and their attendants. These rules are not ignored, and it is a tribute to the intelligence of the cat to see how carefully pussy can become amenable to discipline, if once given to understand of what that discipline consists.

"Then there is a garden cattery. I think this is the prettiest of all. It is covered with roses and ivy. In this there are three rooms, provided with shelves and all other conveniences which can add to the cats' comfort and amusement. The residences of the male cats are most complete, for I have given them every attention possible. Each male cat has his separate sleeping apartments, closed with wire and with a 'run' attached. Close at hand is a large, square grass 'run,' and in this each gentleman takes his daily but solitary exercise. One of the stringent rules of the cattery is that no two males shall ever be left together, and I know that with my cats if this rule were not observed, both in letter and precept, it would be a case of 'when Greek meets Greek.'

"I vary the food for my cats as much as possible. One day we will have most appetizing bowls of fish and rice. At the proper time you can see these standing in the cat kitchen ready to be distributed. Another day these bowls will be filled with minced meat. In the very hot weather a good deal of vegetable matter is mixed with the food. Swiss milk is given, so there is no fear of its turning sour. For some time I have kept a goat on the premises, the milk from which is given to the delicate or younger kittens.

"I have started many of my poorer friends in cat breeding, and they have proved conclusively how easily an addition to their income can be made, not only by breeding good Persian kittens and selling them, but by exhibiting them at the various shows and taking prizes. But of course there is a fashion in cats, as in everything else. When I started breeding blue Persians about fifteen years ago they were very scarce, and I could easily get twenty-five dollars apiece for my kittens. Now this variety is less sought after, and self-silvers, commonly called chinchillas, are in demand."

CHAPTER VII
CONCERNING CAT CLUBS AND CAT SHOWS

The annual cat shows in England, which have been held successively for more than a quarter of a century, led to the establishment in 1887 of a National Cat Club, which has steadily grown in membership and interest, and by the establishment of the National Stud Book and Register has greatly raised the standard of felines in the mother country. It has many well-known people as members, life members, or associates; and from time to time people distinguished in the cat world have been added as honorary members.

The officers of the National Cat Club of England, since its reconstruction in March, 1898, are as follows:--

Presidents.--Her Grace the Duchess of Bedford; Lord Marcus Beresford.

Vice-presidents.--Lily, Duchess of Marlborough, now Lady Wm. Beresford; the Countess of Warwick; Lady Granville Gordon; Hon. Mrs. McL. Morrison; Madame Ronner; Mr. Isaac Woodiwiss; the Countess of Sefton; Lady Hothfield; the Hon. Mrs. Brett; Mr. Sam Woodiwiss; Mr. H.W. Bullock.

President of Committee.--Mr. Louis Wain.

Committee.--Lady Marcus Beresford; Mrs. Balding; Mr. Sidney Woodiwiss; Mr. Hawkins; Mrs. Blair Maconochie; Mrs. Vallance; Mr. Brackett; Mr. F. Gresham.

Hon. Secretary and Hon. Treasurer.--Mrs. Stennard Robinson.

This club has a seal and a motto: "Beauty lives by kindness." It publishes a stud book in which are registered pedigrees and championship wins which are eligible for it. Only wins obtained from shows held under N.C.C. rules are recorded free of charge. The fee for ordinary registration is one shilling per cat, and the stud book is published annually. There are over two thousand cats now entered in this National

Cat Club Stud Book, the form of entry being as follows (L.F. means long-haired female; C.P., Crystal Palace):--

No. 1593, Mimidatzi, L.F. Silver Tabby.
Miss Anna F. Gardner, Hamswell House, near Bath, shown as Mimi.
Bred by Miss How, Bridgeyate, near Bristol. Born April, 1893. Alive.
Sire, Blue Boy the Great of Islington, 1090 (Mrs H.B. Thompson).
Dam, Boots of Bridgeyate, 1225 (Miss How).
Prizes won--1st Bilton, 2nd, C.P. 1893, Kitten Class.

No. 1225, Boots of Bridgeyate. L.F. Silver Tabby.
Miss E. How, Bridgeyate House, Warmly, Bristol.
Former owner, Mrs. Foote, 43 Palace Gardens, Kensington.
Born March, 1892. Alive.

Some of the cats entered have records of prizes covering nearly half a page of the book. The advantage of such a book to cat owners can be readily seen. A cat once entered never changes its number, no matter how many owners he may have, and his name cannot be changed after December 31 of the year in which he is registered.

The more important rules of the English National Cat Club are given in condensed form as follows:--

The name is "The National Cat Club."

Objects: To promote honesty in the breeding of cats, so as to insure purity in each distinct breed or variety; to determine the classification required, and to insure the adoption of such classification by breeders, exhibitors, judges, and the committees of all cat shows; to encourage showing and breeding by giving championship and other prizes, and otherwise doing all in its power to protect and advance the interest of cats and their owners. The National Cat Club shall frame a separate set of rules for cat shows to be called "National Cat Club Rules," and the committees of those cat shows to which the rules are given, shall be called upon to sign a guarantee to the National Cat Club binding them to provide good penning and effectual sanitation, also to the punctual payment of prize money and to the proper adjudication of prizes.

Stud Book: The National Cat Club shall keep a stud book.

Neuter Classes.--For gelded cats.

Kitten Classes.--Single entries over three and under eight months.

Kitten Brace.--Kittens of any age.

Brace.--For two cats of any age.

Team.--For three or more cats, any age.

In Paris, although cats have not been commonly appreciated as in England, there is an increasing interest in them, and cat shows are now a regular feature of the Jardin d'Acclimation. This suggests the subject of the cat's social position in France. Since the Revolution the animal has conquered in this country "toutes les liberties," excepting that of wearing an entire tail, for in many districts it is the fashion to cut the caudal appendage short.

In Paris cats are much cherished wherever they can be without causing too much unpleasantness with the landlord. The system of living in flats is not favorable to cat culture, for the animal, not having access either to the tiles above or to the gutter below, is apt to pine for fresh air, and the society of its congeners. Probably in no other city do these creatures lie in shop windows and on counters with such an arrogant air of proprietorship. In restaurants, a very large and fat cat is kept as an advertisement of the good feeding to be obtained on the premises. There is invariably a cat in a ***charbonnier's*** shop, and the animal is generally one that was originally white, but long ago came to the conclusion that all attempts to keep itself clean were hopeless. Its only consolation is that it is never blacker than its master. It is well known that the Persians and Angoras are much esteemed in Paris and are, to some extent, bred for sale. In the provinces, French cats are usually low-bred animals, with plebeian heads and tails, the stringlike appearance of the latter not being improved by cropping. Although not generally esteemed as an article of food in France, there are still many people scattered throughout the country who maintain that a ***civet de chat*** is as good, or better, than a ***civet de lievre***.

M. Francois Coppee's fondness for cats as pets is so well known that there was great fitness in placing his name first upon the jury of awards at the 1896 cat show in Paris. Such other well-known men as Emile Zola, Andre Theuriet, and Catulle Mendes, also figured on the list. There is now an annual "Exposition Feline Internationale."

In this country the first cat show of general interest was held at Madison Square Garden, New York, in May, 1895. Some years before, there had been a cat show under the auspices of private parties in Boston, and several minor shows had been held at Newburgh, N.Y., and other places. But the New York shows were the first to attract general attention. One hundred and seventy-six cats were exhibited by one hundred and twenty-five owners, besides several ocelots, wild cats, and civets. For some reason the show at Madison Square Garden in March, 1896, catalogued only one hundred and thirty-two cats and eighty-two owners. Since that time there have been no large cat shows in New York.

There have been several cat shows in Boston since 1896, but these are so far only adjuncts to poultry and pigeon shows. Great interest has been manifest in them, however, and the entries have each year run above a hundred. Some magnificent cats are exhibited, although as a rule the animals shown are somewhat small, many kittens being placed there for sale by breeders.

Several attempts to start successful cat clubs in this country have been made. At the close of the New York show in 1896, an American Cat Club was organized for the purpose "of investigating, ascertaining, and keeping a record of the pedigrees of cats, and of instituting, maintaining, controlling, and publishing a stud book, or book of registry of such kind of domestic animals in the United States of America and Canada, and of promoting and holding exhibitions of such animals, and generally for the purpose of improving the breed thereof, and educating the public in its knowledge of the various breeds and varieties of cats."

The officers were as follows:--

President.--Rush S. Huidekoper, 154 E. 57th St., New York City.

Vice-presidents.--W.D. Mann, 208 Fifth Ave., New York City; Mrs. E.N. Barker, Newburgh, N.Y.

Secretary-treasurer.--James T. Hyde, 16 E. 23d St., New York City.

Executive Committee.--T. Farrar Rackham, E. Orange, N.J.; Miss Edith Newbold, Southampton, L.I.; Mrs. Harriet C. Clarke, 154 W. 82d St., New York City; Charles R. Pratt, St. James Hotel, New York City; Joseph W. Stray, 229 Division St., Brooklyn, N.Y.

More successful than this club, however, is the Beresford Cat Club formed in Chicago in the winter of 1899. The president is Mrs. Clinton Locke, who is a member of the English cat clubs, and whose kennel in Chicago contains some of the finest cats in America. The Beresford Cat Club has the sanction of John G. Shortall, of the American Humane Society, and on its honorary list are Miss Agnes Repplier, Madame Ronner, Lady Marcus Beresford, Miss Helen Winslow, and Mr. Louis Wain.

At their cat shows, which are held annually, prizes are offered for all classes of cats, from the common feline of the back alley up to the aristocratic resident of milady's boudoir.

The Beresford Club Cat shows are the most successful of any yet given in America. One hundred and seventy-eight prizes were awarded in the show of January, 1900, and some magnificent cats were shown. It is said by those who are in a position to know that there are no better cats shown in England now than can be seen at the Beresford Show in Chicago. The exhibits cover short and long haired cats of all colors, sizes, and ages, with Siamese cats, Manx cats, and Russian cats. At the show in January, 1900, Mrs. Clinton Locke exhibited fourteen cats of one color, and Mrs. Josiah Cratty five white cats. This club numbers one hundred and seventy members and has a social position and consequent strength second to none in America. It is a fine, honorable club, which has for its objects the protection of the Humane Society and the caring for all cats reported as homeless or in distress. It aims also to establish straightforward and honest dealings among the catteries and to do away with the humbuggery which prevails in some quarters about the sales and valuation of high-bred cats. This club cannot fail to be of great benefit to such as want to carry on an honest industry by the raising and sale of fine cats. It will also improve the breeding of cats in this country, and thereby raise the standard and promote a more general intelligence among the people with regard to cats. Some of the best people in the United States belong to the Beresford Club, the membership of which is by no means confined to Chicago; on the contrary, the club is a national one and the officers and board of directors are:--

President.--Mrs. Clinton Locke.

1st Vice-president.--Mrs W. Eames Colburn.

2d Vice-president.--Mrs. F.A. Howe.

Corresponding Secretary.--Mrs. Henry C. Clark.

Recording Secretary.--Miss Lucy Claire Johnstone.

Treasurer.--Mrs. Charles Hampton Lane.

Mrs. Elwood H. Tolman.

Mrs. J.H. Pratt.

Mrs. Mattie Fisk Green.

Mrs. F.A. Story.

Miss Louise L. Fergus.

The club is anxious to have members all over the United States, just as the English cat clubs do. The non-resident annual fees are only one dollar, and a member has to be proposed by one and endorsed by two other members. The register cats for the stud book are entered at one dollar each, and it is proposed to give shows once a year. The main objects of the club are to improve the breeds of fancy cats in America, to awaken a more general interest in them, and to secure better treatment for the ordinary common cat. The shows will be given for the benefit of the Humane Society.

The Chicago Cat Club has done excellent work also, having established a cat home, or refuge, for stray, homeless, or diseased cats, with a department for boarding pet cats during the absence of their owners. It is under the personal care and direction of Dr. C.A. White, 78 E. 26th Street. The first cat to be admitted there was one from Cleveland, Ohio, which was to be boarded for three months during the absence of its owner in Europe and also to be treated for disease. This club was incorporated under the state laws of Illinois, on January 26, 1899. In connection with it is a children's cat club, which has for its primary object the teaching of kindness to animals by awakening in the young people an appreciative love for cats. At the show of the Chicago Cat Club, small dogs and cavies are exhibited also, the Cavy Club and the Pet Dog Club having affiliated with the Chicago Cat Club.

The president of the Chicago Cat Club is Mrs. Leland Norton, of the Drexel Kennels, at 4011 Drexel Boulevard, Chicago. The corresponding secretary is Mrs. Laura Daunty Pelham, 315 Interocean Building, and the other officers are: Vice-president, Miss Gertrude Estabrooks; recording secretary, Miss Jennie Van Allen; and treasurer, Mrs. Ella B. Shepard. Membership is only one dollar a year, and the registration fee in the Chicago stud book fifty cents for each cat.

The cat shows already held and the flourishing state of our cat clubs have proved that America has as fine, if not finer, cats than can be found in England, and that interest in finely bred cats is on the increase in this country. The effect of the successful cat clubs and cat shows must be to train intelligent judges and to raise the standard of cats in this country. It will also tend to make the cat shows of such a character that kind-hearted owners need not hesitate to enter their choicest cats. As yet, however, the judging at cat shows is not so well managed as in England. It should be a rule that the judges of cats should not only understand their fine points, but should be in sympathy with the little pets.

Cat dealers who have a number of cats entered for competition, should not be allowed on the board of judges. In England, the cats to be judged are taken by classes into a tent for the purpose, and the door is fastened against all but the judges; whereas over here the cats are too often taken out of their cages in the presence of a crowd of spectators and judged on a table or some public place, thereby frightening the timid ones and bringing annoyance to the owners.

Again, there should be several judges. In England there are seven, including two or three women, and these are assigned to different classes: Mr. Harrison Weir, F.R.H.S., the well-known authority on cats, and Louis Wain, the well-known cat artist, are among them. In this country there are a number of women who are not dealers, but who are fully posted in the necessary qualifications for a high-bred cat. American cat shows should have at least three judges, one of whom, at least, should be a woman. A cat should be handled gently and kept as calm as possible during the judging. Women are naturally more gentle in their methods, and more tender-hearted. When my pets are entered for competition, may some wise, kind woman have the judging of them!

In judging a cat the quality and quantity of its fur is the first thing considered. In a long-haired cat this includes the "lord mayor's chain," or frill, the tail, and, most important of all, the ear-tufts. The tufts between the toes and the flexibility of the tail are other important points. The shape of head, eyes, and body are also carefully noted. A short-haired cat is judged first for color, then for eyes, head, symmetry, and ears.

In all cats the head should show breadth between the eyes. The eyes should be round and open. White cats to be really valuable should have blue eyes (without deafness); black cats should have yellow eyes; other cats should have pea-green eyes, or in some cases, as in the brown, self-colored eyes. The nose should be short and tapering. The teeth should be good, and the claws flat. The lower leg should be straight, and the upper hind leg lie at closed angles. The foot should be small and round (in the maltese, pointed). A good cat has a light frame, but a deep chest; a slim, graceful, and fine neck; medium-sized ears with rounded tips. The croup should be square and high; the tail of a short-haired cat long and tapering, and of a long-haired cat broad and bent over at the end.

The good results of a cat show are best told in a few words by one who has acted as judge at an American exhibition.

"One year," he said, "people have to learn that there is such a thing as a cat; the next they come to the show and learn to tell the different breeds; another year they learn the difference between a good cat and a poor one; and the next year they become exhibitors, and tell the judges how to award the premiums."

CHAPTER VIII
CONCERNING HIGH-BRED CATS IN AMERICA

One of the first American women to start a "cattery" in this country was Mrs. Clinton Locke, wife of the rector of Grace Church, Chicago. As a clergyman's wife she has done a great deal of good among the various charities of her city simply from the income derived from her kennels. She has been very generous in gifts of her kittens to other women who have made the raising of fine cats a means to add to a slender income, and has sent beautiful cats all over the United States, to Mexico, and even to Germany. Under her hospitable roof at 2825 Indiana Avenue is a cat family of great distinction. First, there is The Beadle, a splendid blue male with amber eyes, whose long pedigree appears in the third volume of the N.C.C.S.B. under the number 1872, sired by Glaucus, and his dam was Hawthorne Bounce. His pedigree is traced for many generations. He was bred by Mrs. Dean of Hawthornedene, Slough, England. The Beadle took first prize at the cat show held in Chicago in 1896. He also had honorable mention at two cat shows in England when a kitten, under the name of Bumble Bee. Lord Gwynne is a noble specimen, a long-haired white cat with wonderful blue eyes. He was bred from Champion Bundle, and his mother was out of The Masher, No. 1027, winner of many championships. His former owner was Mrs. Davies, of Upper Cattesham. Mrs. Locke purchased him from A.A. Clarke, one of the best judges of cats in England. Lord Gwynne took a prize at the Brighton Cat Show in England in 1895, as a kitten. The father of The Beadle's mate, Rosalys, was the famous "Bluebeard."

Mrs. Locke's chinchillas are the finest ones in this country. Atossa, the mother cat, has a wonderful litter of kittens. She was bred to Lord Argent, one of the three celebrated stud chinchillas in England. She arrived in this country in July, and ten days after gave birth to her foreign kittens. One of the kittens has been sold to Mrs.

Dr. Forsheimer, of Cincinnati, and another to Mrs. W.E. Colburn, of South Chicago. The others Mrs. Locke will not part with at any price.

Smerdis, the grand chinchilla male brought over as a future mate for Atossa, is a royal cat. He looks as though he had run away from Bengal, but, like all of Mrs. Locke's cats, he is gentle and loving. He is the son of Lord Southampton, the lightest chinchilla stud in England (N.C.C.S.B. 1690), and his mother is Silver Spray, No. 1542. His maternal grandparents are Silver King and Harebell, and his great-grandparents Perso and Beauty,--all registered cats. On his father's side a pedigree of three generations can be traced. One of her more recent importations is Lord Gwynne's mate, Lady Mertice, a beautiful long-haired cat with blue eyes. Other famous cats of hers have been Bettina, Nora, Doc, Vashti, Marigold, Grover, and Wendell.

One of Mrs Locke's treasures is a **bona fide** cat mummy, brought by Mrs. Locke from Egypt. It has been verified at the Gizeh Museum to be four thousand years old.

It is fully twenty-five years since Mrs. Locke began to turn her attention to fine cats, and when she imported her first cat to Chicago there was only one other in the United States. That one was Mrs. Edwin Brainard's Madam, a wonderful black, imported from Spain. Her first long-haired cat was Wendell, named for the friend who brought him from Persia, and his descendants are now in the Lockehaven Cattery. Queen Wendella is one of the most famous cats in America to-day, and mother of the beautiful Lockehaven Quartette. These are all descended from the first Wendell. The kittens in the Lockehaven Quartette went to Mrs. S.S. Leach, Bonny Lea, New London, Ct.; Miss Lucy Nichols, Ben Mahr Cattery, Waterbury, Ct.; Miss Olive Watson, Warrensburg, Pa.; and Mrs. B.M. Gladding, at Memphis, Tenn, Mrs. Locke's Lord Argent, descended from Atossa and the famous Lord Argent, of England, is a magnificent cat, while her Smerdis is the son of the greatest chinchillas in the world. Rosalys II, now owned by Mr. C.H. Jones, of Palmyra, N.Y., was once her cat, and was the daughter of Rosalys (owned by Miss Nichols, of Waterbury, Ct), who was a granddaughter of the famous Bluebeard, of England. These, with the beautiful brown tabby, Crystal, owned by Mr. Jones, have all been prize winners. Lucy Claire is a recent importation, who won second and third prizes in England under the name of Baby Flossie. She is the daughter of Duke of Kent and Topso, of Merevale. Her paternal grandparents are Mrs. Herring's well-known champion, Blue Jack, and Marney. The maternal grandparents are King Harry, a prize winner at Clifton and Brighton, and Fluff.

Mrs. Locke's cats are all imported. She has sometimes purchased cats from Maine or elsewhere for people who did not care to pay the price demanded for her fine kittens, but she has never had in her own cattery any cats of American origin. Her stock, therefore, is probably the choicest in America. She always has from twenty to twenty-five cats, and the cat-lover who obtains one of her kittens is fortunate indeed. A beautiful pair of blacks in Mrs. Locke's cattery have the most desirable shade of amber eyes, and are named "Blackbird" and "St. Tudno"; she has also a choice pair of Siamese cats called "Siam" and "Sally Ward."

Mrs. Josiah Cratty, of Oak Park, has a cattery called the "Jungfrau Katterie," and her cats are remarkably beautiful. Her Bartimaeus and True Blue are magnificent white cats, sired by Mrs. Locke's Lord Gwynne.

Miss L.C. Johnstone, of Chicago, has some of the handsomest cats in the country. Cherie is a wonderful blue shaded cat; Lord Humm is a splendid brown tabby; while Beauty Belle is an exceedingly handsome white cat. Miss Johnstone takes great pains with her cats, and is rewarded by having them rated among the best in America.

Some of the beautiful cats which have been sent from Chicago to homes elsewhere are Teddy Roosevelt, a magnificent white, sired by Mrs. W.E. Colburn's Paris, and belonging to Mrs. L. Kemp, of Huron, S. Dak.; Silver Dick, a gorgeous buff and white, whose grandmother was Mrs. Colburn's Caprice, and who is owned by Mrs. Porter L. Evans, of East St. Louis; Toby, a pure white with green eyes, owned by Mrs. Elbert W. Shirk, of Indianapolis; and Amytis, a chinchilla belonging to Mrs. S.S. Leach, of New London, sired by Mrs. Locke's Smerdis, and the daughter of Rosalys II.

Miss Cora Wallace, of East Brady, Pa., has Lord Ruffles, son of the first Rosalys and The Beadle, formerly Bumble Bee. Mrs. Fisk Greene, of Chicago, now owns a beautiful cat in Bumble Bee, and another in Miss Merrylegs, a blue with golden eyes, the daughter of Bumble Bee and Black Sapho. The Misses Peacock, of Topeka, have a pair of whites called Prince Hilo and Rosebud, the latter having blue eyes. Mrs. Frederick Monroe, of Riverside, Ill., owns a remarkable specimen of a genuine Russian cat, a perfect blue of extraordinary size. Miss Elizabeth Knight, of Milwaukee, has a beautiful silver tabby, Winifred, the daughter of Whychwood, Miss Kate Loraine Gage's celebrated silver tabby, of Brewster, N.Y. The most perfect "lavender blue" cat belongs to Miss Lucy E. Nichols, of Waterbury, Ct., and is named Roscal. He has beautiful long fur, with a splendid ruff and tail, and is a son of Rosalys and The Beadle.

Mrs. Leland Norton has a number of magnificent cats. It was she who adopted Miss Frances Willard's "Tootsie," the famous cat which made two thousand dollars for the temperance cause. Miss Nella B. Wheatley has very fine kennels, and raises some beautiful cats. Her Taffy is a beautiful buff and white Angora, which has been very much admired. Her cats have been sold to go to many other cities. Speaking from her own experience Miss Wheatley says, "Raising Angoras is one of the most fascinating of employments, and I have found, when properly taken care of, they are among the most beautiful, strong, intelligent, and playful of all animals."

Mrs. W.E. Colburn is another very successful owner of cat kennels. She has had some of the handsomest cats in this country, among which are "Paris," a magnificent white cat with blue eyes, and his mother, "Caprice," who has borne a number of wonderfully fine pure white Angoras with the most approved shade of blue eyes. Her cattery is known as the "Calumet Kennel," and there is no better judge of cats in the country than Mrs. Colburn.

So much has been said of the cats which were "mascots" on the ships during the Cuban War that it is hardly necessary to speak of them. Tom, the mascot of the *Maine*, and Christobal have been shown in several cities of the Union since the war.

The most beautiful collection of brown tabbies is owned by Mr. C.H. Jones, of Palmyra, N.Y., who has the "Crystal Cattery." Crystal, the son of Mrs. E.M. Barker's "King Humbert," is the champion brown tabby of America, and is a magnificent creature, of excellent disposition and greatly admired by cat fanciers everywhere. Mona Liza, his mate, and Goozie and Bubbles make up as handsome a quartet of this variety as one could wish to see. Goozie's tail is now over twelve inches in circumference. Mr. Jones keeps about twenty fine cats in stock all the time.

The most highly valued cat in America is Napoleon the Great, whose owner has refused four thousand dollars for him. A magnificent fellow he is too, with his bushy orange fur and lionlike head. He is ten years old and weighs twenty-three pounds, which is a remarkable weight in a male cat, only gelded ones ordinarily running above fifteen pounds. Napoleon was bred by a French nobleman, and was born at the Chateau Fontainebleau, near Paris, in 1888. He is a pure French Angora, which is shown by his long crinkly hair--so long that it has to be frequently clipped to preserve the health and comfort of the beautiful creature. This clipping is what causes the uneven quality of fur which appears in his picture. His mother was a famous cat, and his grandmother was one of the grandest dams of France (no pun intended). The latter lived to be nineteen years old, and consequently Napoleon the Great is regarded by his owners as a mere youth. He has taken first prizes and medals wherever he has been exhibited, and at Boston, 1897, won the silver cup offered for the best cat in the exhibition.

Another fine cat belonging to Mrs. Weed, is Marguerite, mother of Le Noir, a beautiful black Angora, sired by Napoleon the Great and owned by Mrs. Weed. Juno is Napoleon's daughter, born in 1894, and is valued at fifteen hundred dollars. When she was seven months old her owners refused two hundred dollars for her. She is a tortoise-shell and white French Angora, and a remarkably beautiful creature. All these cats are great pets, and are allowed the freedom of the house and barns, although when they run about the grounds there is always a man in attendance. Six or seven thousand dollars' worth of cats sporting on the lawn together is a rich sight, but not altogether without risk.

Mrs. Fabius M. Clarke's "Persia," a beautiful dark chinchilla, is one of the finest cats in this country. She began her career by taking special and first prizes at Fastmay's Cat Show in England, as the best long-haired kitten. She also took the first prize as a kitten at Lancashire, and at the National Cat Show in New York in 1895. She was bred in England; sire, King of Uhn; dam, Brunette, of pure imported Persian stock. Mrs. Clarke brought her home in January, 1895, and she is still worshipped as a family pet at her New York home. "Sylvio" was also brought over at the same time. He was a beautiful long-haired male silver tabby, and bred by Mrs. A.F. Gardner. Sylvio was sired by the famous Topso of Dingley (owned by Miss Leake), famous as the best long-haired tabby in England. Sylvio's mother was Mimidatzi, whose pedigree is given in the previous chapter. "Mimi's" sire was the champion Blue Boy the Great, whose mother was Boots of Bridgeyate, whose pedigree is also given in the extract from the stud book. Sylvio took a first prize at the New York Show, 1895, but unfortunately was poisoned before he was a year old. This seems the greater pity, because he had a remarkably fine pedigree, and gave promise of being one of the best cats America has yet seen.

Persia is a handsome specimen of the fine blue chinchilla class. She is quiet, amiable, and shows her high breeding in her good manners and intelligence. Her tail is like a fox's brush, and her ruff gladdens the heart of every cat fancier that beholds her. She is an aristocratic little creature, and seems to feel that she comes of famous foreign ancestry. Mrs. Clarke makes great pets of her beautiful cats, and trains them to do many a cunning trick.

Another cat which has won several prizes, and took the silver bowl offered for the best cat and litter of kittens in the 1895 cat show of New York is Ellen Terry, a handsome orange and white, exhibited by Mrs. Fabius M. Clarke. At that show she had seven beautiful kittens, and they all reposed in a dainty white and yellow basket with the mother, delighting the hearts of all beholders. She now belongs to Mrs. Brian Brown, of Brooklyn. She is a well-bred animal, with a pretty face and fine feathering. One of the kittens who won the silver bowl in 1895 took the second prize for long-haired white female in New York, in March, 1896. She is a beautiful creature, known as Princess Dinazarde, and belongs to Mrs. James S.H. Umsted, of New York.

Sylvia is still in Mrs. Clarke's possession, and is a beautiful creature, dainty, refined, and very jealous of her mistress's affection. Mrs. Clarke also owns a real Manx cat, brought from the Isle of Man by Captain McKenzie. It acts like a monkey, climbing up on mantels and throwing down pictures and other small objects, in the regular monkey spirit of mischief. It has many queer attributes, and hops about like a rabbit. She also owns Sapho, who was bred by Ella Wheeler Wilcox from her Madame Ref and Mr. Stevens's Ajax, an uncommonly handsome white Angora.

The sire of Topso and Sylvia was Musjah, owned by Mr. Ferdinand Danton, a New York artist. He was a magnificent creature, imported from Algiers in 1894; a pure blue Persian of uncommon size and beautiful coloring. Musjah was valued at two hundred dollars, but has been stolen from Mr. Danton. Probably his present owner will not exhibit him at future cat shows.

Ajax is one of the finest white Angoras in this country. His owner, Mr. D.W.

Stevens, of West-field, Mass., has refused five hundred dollars for him, and would not consider one thousand dollars as a fair exchange for the majestic creature. He was born in 1893, and is valued, not only for his fine points, but because he is a family pet, with a fine disposition and uncommon intelligence. At the New York show in 1895, and at several other shows, he has won first prizes.

One of his sons bids fair to be as fine a cat as Ajax. This is Sampson, bred by Ella Wheeler Wilcox, from Madame Ref, and owned by Mrs. Brian Brown. Mr. Stevens has a number of other high-bred cats, one of whom is Raby, a reddish black female, with a red ruff. Another is Lady, who is pure white; and then there are Monkey and Midget, who are black and white Angoras. All of these cats are kept in a pen, half of which is within the barn, and the other half out of doors and enclosed by wire netting. Ajax roams over the house at will, and the others pass some of the time there, but the entire collection, sometimes numbering twenty-five, is too valuable to be given the freedom of all outdoors. Both Mr. and Mrs. Stevens are very fond of cats, and have made a study of them in sickness and health. Some years ago, a malicious raid was made on the pen, and every cat poisoned with the exception of Raby, whose life was saved only by frequent and generous doses of skunk's oil and milk.

At the first New York show, Miss Ethel Nesmith Anderson's Chico, an imported Persian, took the second prize, after Ajax, in the pure white, longhaired class. The third prize was won by Snow, another imported Angora, belonging to Mr. George A. Rawson, of Newton, Mass. Snow had already taken a prize at Crystal Palace. He is a magnificent animal. Mr. Rawson owns a number of beautiful cats, which are the pride of his family, and bring visitors from all parts of the country. His orange-colored, long-haired Dandy won first prizes at the Boston shows of 1896 and 1897 in the gelded class. He is beautifully marked, and has a disposition as "childlike and bland" as the most exacting owner could wish. Miss Puff is also owned by Mr. Rawson, and presents him with beautiful white Angora kittens every year. The group of ten white kittens, raised by him in 1896, gives some idea of the beauty of these kittens: although the picture was taken with a high wind blowing in their faces, causing one white beauty to conceal all marks of identification except an ear, and another to hide completely behind his playmates.

Mustapha was entered by Dr. Huidekoper in the first New York show, but not for competition. He was a magnificent brindled Persian gelded cat, six years old, who enjoyed the plaudits of the multitude just as well as though he had taken first prize. He was very fond of his master, but very shy with strangers when at home. He slept on the library desk, or a cushion next his master's bed whenever he could be alone with the doctor, but at other times preferred his own company or that of the cook.

Another cat that attracted a great deal of attention was Master Pettet's Tommy, a white Persian, imported in 1889 and valued at five hundred dollars, although no money consideration could induce his owners to part with him. He was brought from the interior of Persia, where he was captured in a wild state. He was kept caged for over a year, and would not be tamed; but at last he became domesticated, and is now one of the dearest pets imaginable. His fur is extremely long and soft, without a colored hair. His tail is broad and carried proudly aloft, curling over toward his back when walking. His face is full of intelligence: his ears well-tipped and feathered, and his ruff a thing of beauty and a joy forever.

King Max, a long-haired, black male, weighing thirteen pounds at the age of one year, and valued at one thousand dollars, took first prizes in Boston in January, 1897, '98, and '99. He is owned by Mrs. E.R. Taylor, of Medford, Mass., and attracts constant attention during shows. His fur is without a single white hair and is a finger deep; his ruff encircles his head like a great aureole. He is not only one of the most beautiful cats I have ever seen, but one of the best-natured: as his reputation for beauty spreads among visitors at the show, everybody wants to see him, and he has no chance at all for naps. Generally he is brought forward and taken from his cage a hundred times a day; but not once does he show the least sign of ill-temper, and even on the last day of the show he keeps up a continual low purr of content and happiness. Perhaps he knows how handsome he is.

Grover B., the Mascotte, is a Philadelphia cat who took the twenty-five dollar gold medal in 1895, at the New York show, as the heaviest white cat exhibited. He belongs to Mr. and Mrs. W.P. Buchanan, and weighs over twenty pounds. He is a thoroughbred, and is valued at one thousand dollars, having been brought from the Isle of Malta, and he wears a one-hundred-dollar gold collar. He is a remarkable cat, noted particularly for his intelligence and amiability. He is very dainty in his choice of food, and prefers to eat his dinners in his high chair at the table. He has a fascinating habit of feeding himself with his paws. He is very talkative just before mealtimes, and is versed in all the feline arts of making one's self understood. He waits at the front door for his master every night, and will not leave him all the evening. He sleeps in a bed of his own, snugly wrapped up in blankets, and he is admired by all who know him, not more for his beauty than for his excellent deportment. He furnishes one more proof that a properly trained and well-cared-for cat has a large amount of common sense and appreciation.

Mrs. Frances Hodgson Burnett's tiger cat Dick attracted a great deal of attention at the first New York show. He weighs twenty-two pounds and is three feet long, with a girth of twenty-four inches; and he has attained some degree of prominence in her writings.

A trio of cats that were a centre of attraction at that first show belonged to Colonel Mann, of **Town Topics**. They were jet black, and rejoiced in the names of Taffy, The Laird, and Little Billee. They took a first prize, but two of them have since come to an untimely end. Colonel Mann is a devoted lover of animals, and has given a standing order that none of his employees shall, if they see a starving kitten on the street, leave it to suffer and die. Accordingly his office is a sort of refuge for unfortunate cats, and one may always see a number of happy-looking creatures there, who seem to appreciate the kindness which surrounds them. The office is in a fifth story overlooking Fifth Avenue: and the cats used to crawl out on the wide window-ledge in summer-time and enjoy the air and the view of Madison Square. But alas! The Laird and Little Billee came to their deaths by jumping from their high perch after sparrows and falling to the pavement below. Now there is a strong wire grating across the windows, and Taffy, a monstrous, shiny black fellow, is the leader in the "Town Topics Colony."

Dr. H.L. Hammond, of Killingly, Ct., makes a speciality of the rare Australian cats, and has taken numerous prizes with them at every cat show in this country, where they are universally admired. His Columbia is valued at six hundred dollars, and his Tricksey at five hundred dollars. They are, indeed, beautiful creatures, though somewhat unique in the cat world, as we see it. They are very sleek cats, with fur so short, glossy, and fine that it looks like the finest satin. Their heads are small and narrow, with noses that seem pointed when compared with other cats. They are very intelligent and affectionate little creatures, and make the loveliest of pets. Dr. and Mrs. Hammond are extremely fond of their unusual and valuable cat family,--and tell the most interesting tales of their antics and habits. His Columbia was an imported cat, and the doctor has reason to believe that she with her mate are originally from the Siamese cat imported from Siam to Australia. They are all very delicate as kittens, the mother rarely having more than one at a time. With two exceptions, these cats have never had more than two kittens at a litter. They are very partial to heat, but cannot stand cold weather. They have spells of sleeping when nothing has power to disturb them, but when they do wake up they have a "high time," running and playing. They are affectionate, being very fond of their owner, but rather shy with strangers. They are uncommonly intelligent, too, and are very teachable when young. They are such beautiful creatures, besides being rare in this part of the world, that it is altogether probable that they will be much sought after as pets.

CHAPTER IX
CONCERNING CATS IN POETRY

As far back as the ninth century, a poem on a cat was written, which has come down to us from the Arabic. Its author was Ibn Alalaf Alnaharwany, of Bagdad, who died in 318 A.H. or A.D. 930. He was one of the better known poets of the khalifate, and his work may still be found in the original. The following verses, which were translated by Dr. Carlyle, are confessedly a paraphrase rather than a strict translation; but, of course, the sense is the same. Commentators differ on the question as to whether the poet really meant anything more in this poem than to sing of the death of a pet, and some have tried to ascribe to it a hidden meaning which implies beautiful slaves, lovers, and assignations; just as the wise Browning student discovers meanings in that great poet's works of which he never dreamed. Nevertheless, we who love cats are fain to believe that this follower of Mahomet meant only to celebrate the merits--perhaps it would hardly do to call them virtues--of his beloved cat.

The lines are inscribed,--

ON A CAT

THAT WAS KILLED AS SHE WAS ATTEMPTING TO ROB A DOVE-HOUSE

BY IBN ALALAF ALNAHARWANY

Poor Puss is gone!--'tis Fate's decree--
Yet I must still her loss deplore;

For dearer than a child was she,
  And ne'er shall I behold her more!

With many a sad, presaging tear,
  This morn I saw her steal away,
While she went on without a fear,
  Except that she should miss her prey.

I saw her to the dove-house climb,
  With cautious feet and slow she stept,
Resolved to balance loss of time
  By eating faster than she crept.

Her subtle foes were on the watch,
  And marked her course, with fury fraught;
And while she hoped the birds to catch,
  An arrow's point the huntress caught.

In fancy she had got them all,
  And drunk their blood and sucked their breath;
Alas! she only got a fall,
  And only drank the draught of death.

Why, why was pigeon's flesh so nice,
  That thoughtless cats should love it thus?
Hadst thou but lived on rats and mice,
  Thou hadst been living still, poor Puss!

Cursed be the taste, howe'er refined,
  That prompts us for such joys to wish;
And cursed the dainty where we find
  Destruction lurking in the dish.

Among the poets, Pussy has always found plenty of friends. Her feline grace and softness has inspired some of the greatest, and, from Tasso and Petrarch down, her quiet and dignified demeanor have been celebrated in verse. Mr. Swinburne, within a few years, has written a charming poem which was published in the **Athenaeum**, and which places the writer among the select inner circle of true cat-lovers. He calls his verses--

TO A CAT

Stately, kindly, lordly friend,
  Condescend
Here to sit by me, and turn
Glorious eyes that smile and burn,
Golden eyes, love's lustrous meed,
On the golden page I read.

  *   *   *   *   *

Dogs may fawn on all and some
  As they come:
You a friend of loftier mind,
Answer friends alone in kind.
Just your foot upon my hand
Softly bids it understand.

Thomas Gray's poem on the death of Robert Walpole's cat, which was drowned in a bowl of goldfish, was greatly prized by the latter; after the death of the poet the bowl was placed on a pedestal at Strawberry Hill, with a few lines from the poem as an inscription. In a letter dated March 1, 1747, accompanying it, Mr. Gray says:--
"As one ought to be particularly careful to avoid blunders in a compliment of condolence, it would be a sensible satisfaction to me (before I testify my sorrow and the sincere part I take in your misfortune) to know for certain who it is I lament. [Note the 'Who.'] I knew Zara and Selima (Selima was it, or Fatima?), or rather I

knew them both together, for I cannot justly say which was which. Then, as to your handsome cat, the name you distinguish her by, I am no less at a loss, as well knowing one's handsome cat is always the cat one likes best; or if one be alive and the other dead, it is usually the latter that is the handsomest. Besides, if the point were never so clear, I hope you do not think me so ill bred or so imprudent as to forfeit all my interest in the survivor. Oh, no; I would rather seem to mistake and imagine, to be sure, it must be the tabby one that had met with this sad accident. Till this affair is a little better determined, you will excuse me if I do not cry, 'Tempus inane peto, requiem, spatiumque doloris.'"

He closes the letter by saying, "There's a poem for you; it is rather too long for an epitaph." And then the familiar--

    "'Twas on a lofty vase's side,
    Where China's gayest art had dy'd
      The azure flowers that blow:
    Demurest of the tabby kind,
    The pensive Selima, reclined,
      Gazed on the lake below."

Wordsworth's "Kitten and the Falling Leaves," is in the high, moralizing style.

    "That way look, my Infant, lo!
    What a pretty baby show.
    See the kitten on the wall,
    Sporting with the leaves that fall,

    *   *   *   *   *

    "But the kitten, how she starts,
    Crouches, stretches, paws, and darts
    First at one and then its fellow,

Just as light and just as yellow:
There are many now--now one,
Now they stop, and there are none.
What intentness of desire
In her upward eye of fire!
With a tiger-leap halfway
Now she meets the coming prey,
Lets it go as fast, and then
Has it in her power again:
Now she works with three or four.
Like an Indian conjuror:
Quick as he in feats of art,
Far beyond in joy of heart.
Were her antics played in the eye
Of a thousand standers-by,
Clapping hands with shout and stare,
What would little Tabby care
For the plaudits of the crowd?
Over happy to be proud,
Over wealthy in the treasure
Of her own exceeding pleasure.

    *   *   *   *   *

"Pleased by any random toy:
By a kitten's busy joy,
Or an infant's laughing eye
Sharing in the ecstacy:
I would fain like that or this
Find my wisdom in my bliss:
Keep the sprightly soul awake,
And have faculties to take,
Even from things by sorrow wrought,

Matter for a jocund thought,
Spite of care and spite of grief,
To gambol with life's falling leaf."

Cowper's love for animals was well known. At one time, according to Lady Hesketh, he had besides two dogs, two goldfinches, and two canaries, five rabbits, three hares, two guinea-pigs, a squirrel, a magpie, a jay, and a starling. In addition he had, at least, one cat, for Lady Hesketh says, "One evening the cat giving one of the hares a sound box on the ear, the hare ran after her, and having caught her, punished her by drumming on her back with her two feet hard as drumsticks, till the creature would actually have been killed had not Mrs. Unwin rescued her." It might have been this very cat that was the inspiration of Cowper's poem, "To a Retired Cat," which had as a moral the familiar stanza:--

"Beware of too sublime a sense
Of your own worth and consequence:
The man who dreams himself so great
And his importance of such weight,
That all around, in all that's done,
Must move and act for him alone,
Will learn in school of tribulation
The folly of his expectation."

Baudelaire wrote:--

"Come, beauty, rest upon my loving heart,
But cease thy paws' sharp-nailed play,
And let me peer into those eyes that dart
Mixed agate and metallic ray."

"Grave scholars and mad lovers all admire
And love, and each alike, at his full tide

Those suave and puissant cats, the fireside's pride,
Who like the sedentary life and glow of fire."

Goldsmith also wrote of the kitten:--

"Around in sympathetic mirth
  Its tricks the kitten tries:
The cricket chirrups in the hearth,
  The crackling fagot flies."

Does this not suggest a charming glimpse of the poet's English home?

Keats was evidently not acquainted with the best and sleekest pet cat, and his "Sonnet to a Cat" does not indicate that he fully appreciated their higher qualities.

Mr. Whittier, our good Quaker poet, while not attempting an elaborate sonnet or stilted elegiac, shows a most appreciative spirit in the lines he wrote for a little girl who asked him one day, with tears in her eyes, to write an epitaph for her lost Bathsheba.

"Bathsheba: To whom none ever said scat,
    No worthier cat
    Ever sat on a mat
    Or caught a rat:
    Requies-cat."

Clinton Scollard, however, has given us an epitaph that many sympathizing admirers would gladly inscribe on the tombstones of their lost pets, if it were only the popular fashion to put tombstones over their graves. This is Mr. Scollard's tribute, the best ever written:--

GRIMALKIN

AN ELEGY ON PETER, AGED TWELVE

In vain the kindly call: in vain
The plate for which thou once wast fain
At morn and noon and daylight's wane,
　　O King of mousers.
No more I hear thee purr and purr
As in the frolic days that were,
When thou didst rub thy velvet fur
　　Against my trousers.

How empty are the places where
Thou erst wert frankly debonair,
Nor dreamed a dream of feline care,
　　A capering kitten.
The sunny haunts where, grown a cat,
You pondered this, considered that,
The cushioned chair, the rug, the mat,
　　By firelight smitten.

Although of few thou stoodst in dread,
How well thou knew a friendly tread,
And what upon thy back and head
　　The stroking hand meant.
A passing scent could keenly wake
Thy eagerness for chop or steak,
Yet, Puss, how rarely didst thou break
　　The eighth commandment.

Though brief thy life, a little span
Of days compared with that of man,

The time allotted to thee ran
   In smoother metre.
Now with the warm earth o'er thy breast,
O wisest of thy kind and best,
Forever mayst thou softly rest,
   In pace, Peter.

One only has to read this poem to feel that Mr. Scollard knew what it is to love a gentle, intelligent, affectionate cat--made so by kind treatment.

To Francois Coppee the cat is as sacred as it was to the Egyptians of old. The society of his feline pets is to him ever delightful and consoling, and it may have inspired him to write some of his most melodious verses. Nevertheless he is not the cat's poet. It was Charles Cros who wrote:--

"Chatte blanche, chatte sans tache,
Je te demande dans ces vers
Quel secret dort dans tes yeux verts,
Quel sarcasme sous ta moustache?"

Here is a version in verse of the famous "Kilkenny Cats":--

"O'Flynn, she was an Irishman, as very well was known,
And she lived down in Kilkenny, and she lived there all alone,
With only six great large tom-cats that knowed their ways about;
And everybody else besides she scrupulously shut out."

"Oh, very fond of cats was she, and whiskey, too, 'tis said,
She didn't feed 'em very much, but she combed 'em well instead:
As may be guessed, these large tom-cats did not get very sleek
Upon a combing once a day and a 'haporth' once a week.

"Now, on one dreary winter's night O'Flynn she went to bed
With a whiskey bottle under her arm, the whiskey in her head.

The six great large tom-cats they all sat in a dismal row,
And horridly glared their hazy eyes, their tails wagged to and fro.

"At last one grim graymalkin spoke, in accents dire to tell,
And dreadful were the words which in his horrid whisper fell:
And all the six large tom-cats in answer loud did squall,
'Let's kill her, and let's eat her, body, bones, and all.'

"Oh, horrible! Oh, terrible! Oh, deadly tale to tell!
When the sun shone through the window-hole all seemed still and well:
The cats they sat and licked their paws all in a merry ring.
But nothing else in all the house looked like a living thing.

"Anon they quarrelled savagely--they spit, they swore, they hollered:
At last these six great large tom-cats they one another swallered:
And naught but one long tail was left in that once peaceful dwelling,
And a very tough one, too, it was--it's the same that I've been telling."

By far more artistic is the version for which I am indebted to Miss Katharine Eleanor Conway, herself a poet of high order and a lover of cats.

THE KILKENNY CATS

There wanst was two cats in Kilkenny,
Aitch thought there was one cat too many;
  So they quarrelled and fit,
  They scratched and they bit,
  Till, excepting their nails,
  And the tips of their tails,
Instead of two cats, there wasn't any.

This version comes from Ireland, and is doubtless the correct original.
"Note," says Miss Conway, "the more than Greek delicacy with which the trag-

edy is told. No mutilation, no gore; just an effacement--prompt and absolute--'there wasn't any.' It would be hard to overpraise that fine touch."

CHAPTER X
CONCERNING CAT ARTISTS

While thousands of artists, first and last, have undertaken to paint cats, there are but few who have been able to do them justice. Artists who have possessed the technical skill requisite to such delicate work have rarely been willing to give to what they have regarded as unimportant subjects the necessary study; and those who have been willing to study cats seriously have possessed but seldom the skill requisite to paint them well.

Thomas Janvier, whose judgment on such matters is unquestioned, declares that not a dozen have succeeded in painting thoroughly good cat portraits, portraits so true to nature as to satisfy--if they could express their feelings in the premises--the cat subjects and their cat friends. Only four painters, he says, ever painted cats habitually and always well.

Two members of this small but highly distinguished company flourished about a century ago in widely separated parts of the world, and without either of them knowing that the other existed.

One was a Japanese artist, named Ho-Kou-Say, whose method of painting, of course, was quite unlike that to which we are accustomed in this western part of the world, but who had a wonderful faculty for making his queer little cat figures seem intensely alive.

The other was a Swiss artist, named Gottfried Mind, whose cat pictures are so perfect in their way that he came to be honorably known as "the Cat Raphael."

The other two members of the cat quartet are the French artist, Monsieur Louis Eugene Lambert, whose pictures are almost as well known in this country as they are in France; and the Dutch artist, Madame Henriette Ronner, whose delightful cat pictures are known even better, as she catches the softer and sweeter graces of the cat more truly than Lambert.

A thoroughly good picture of a cat is hard to paint, from a technical standpoint, because the artist must represent not only the soft surface of fur, but the underlying hard lines of muscle: and his studies must be made under conditions of cat perversity which are at times quite enough to drive him wild. If he is to represent the cat in repose, he must wait for her to take that position of her own accord; and then, just as his sketch is well under way, she is liable to rise, stretch herself, and walk off. If his picture is to represent action, he must wait for the cat to do what he wants her to do, and that many times before he can be quite sure that his drawing is correct. With these severe limitations upon cat painting, it is not surprising that very few good pictures of cats have been painted.

Gottfried Mind has left innumerable pen sketches to prove his intimate knowledge of the beauty and charm of the cat. He was born at Berne in 1768. He had a special taste for drawing animals even when very young, bears and cats being his favorite subjects. As he grew older he obtained a wonderful proficiency, and his cat pictures appeared with every variety of expression. Their silky coats, their graceful attitudes, their firm shape beneath the undulating fur, were treated so as to make Mind's cats seem alive.

It was Madame Lebrun who named him the "Raphael of Cats," and many a royal personage bought his pictures. He, like most cat painters, kept his cats constantly with him, knowing that only by persistent and never tiring study could he ever hope to master their infinite variety. His favorite mother cat kept closely at his side when he worked, or perhaps in his lap; while her kittens ran over him as fearlessly as they played with their mother's tail. When a terrible epidemic broke out among the cats of Berne in 1809, he hid his Minette safely from the police, but he never quite recovered from the horror of the massacre of the eight hundred that had to be sacrificed for the general safety of the people. He died in 1814, and in poverty, although a few years afterward his pictures brought extravagant prices.

Burbank, the English painter, has done some good things in cat pictures. The expression of the face and the peculiar light in the cat's eye made up the realism of Burbank's pictures, which were reproductions of sleek and handsome drawing-room pets, whose shining coats he brings out with remarkable precision.

The ill-fated Swiss artist Cornelius Wisscher's marvellous tom-cat has become typical.

Delacroix, the painter of tigers, was a man of highly nervous temperament, but his cat sketches bring out too strongly the tigerish element to be altogether successful.

Louis Eugene Lambert was a pupil of Delacroix. He was born in Paris, September 25, 1825, and the chief event of his youth was, perhaps, the great friendship which existed between him and Maurice Sands. Entomology was a fad with him for a time, but he finally took up his serious life-work in 1854, when he began illustrating for the ***Journal of Agriculture***. In connection with his work, he began to study animals carefully, making dogs his specialty. In 1862 he illustrated an edition of La Fontaine, and in 1865 he obtained his first medal for a painting of dogs. In 1866 his painting of cats, "L'Horloge qui avance," won another medal, and brought his first fame as a cat painter. In 1874 he was made a Chevalier of the Legion of Honor. His "Envoi" in 1874, "Les Chats du Cardinal," and "Grandeur Decline" brought more medals. Although he has painted hosts of excellent dog pictures, cats are his favorites, on account, as he says, of "les formes fines et gracieux; mouvements, souple et subtil."

In the Luxembourg Gallery, Mr. Lambert's "Family of Cats" is considered one of the finest cat pictures in the world. In this painting the mother sits upon a table watching the antics of her four frivolous kittens. There is a wonderful smoothness of touch and refinement of treatment that have never yet been excelled. "After the Banquet" is another excellent example of the same smoothness of execution, with fulness of action instead of repose. And yet there is an undeniable lack of the softer attributes which should be evident in the faces of the group.

It is here that Madame Ronner excels all other cat painters, living or dead. She not only infuses a wonderful degree of life into her little figures, but reproduces the shades of expression, shifting and variable as the sands of the sea, as no other artist of the brush has done. Asleep or awake, her cats look exactly to the "felinarian" like cats with whom he or she is familiar. Curiosity, drowsiness, indifference, alertness, love, hate, anxiety, temper, innocence, cunning, fear, confidence, mischief, earnestness, dignity, helplessness,--they are all in Madame Ronner's cats' faces, just as we see them in our own cats.

Madame Ronner is the daughter of Josephus Augustus Knip, a landscape painter of some celebrity sixty years ago, and from her father she received her first art education. She is now over seventy years old, and for nearly fifty years has made her home in Brussels. There, she and her happy cats, a big black Newfoundland dog named Priam, with a pert cockatoo named Coco, dwell together in a roomy house in its own grounds, back a little from the Charleroi Road. Madame Ronner has a good son to care for her, and she loves the animals, who are both her servants and her friends. Every day she spends three good hours of the morning in her studio, painting her delightful cat pictures with the energy of a young artist and the expert precision which we know so well. She was sixteen when she succeeded in painting a picture which was accepted and sold at a public exhibition at Dusseldorf. This was a study of a cat seated in a window and examining with great curiosity a bumblebee; while it would not compare with her later work, there must have been good quality in it, or it would not have got into a Dusseldorf picture exhibition at all. At any rate, it was the beginning of her successful career as an artist. From that time she managed to support herself and her father by painting pictures of animals. For many years, however, she confined herself to painting dogs. Her most famous picture, "The Friend of Man," belongs to this period--a pathetic group composed of a sorrowing old sand-seller looking down upon a dying dog still harnessed to the little sand-wagon, with the two other dogs standing by with wistful looks of sympathy. When this picture was exhibited, in 1860, Madame Ronner's fame was established permanently.

But it so happened that in the same year a friendly kitten came to live in her home, wandering in through the open doorway from no one knew where, and deciding, after sniffing about the place in cat fashion, to remain there for the remainder of its days. And it also happened that Madame Ronner was lured by this small stranger, who so coolly quartered himself upon her, to change the whole current of her artistic life, and to paint cats instead of dogs. Of course, this change could not be made in a moment; but after that the pictures which she painted to please herself were cat pictures, and as these were exhibited and her reputation as a cat painter became established, cat orders took the place of dog orders more and more, until at last her time was given wholly to cat painting. Her success in painting cat action has been due as much to her tireless patience as to her skill; a patience that gave her strength to spend hours upon hours in carefully watching the quick movements of the lithe little creatures, and in correcting again and again her rapidly made sketches.

Every cat-lover knows that a cat cannot be induced, either by reason or by affection, to act in accordance with any wishes save its own. Also that cats find malicious amusement in doing what they know they are not wanted to do, and that with an affectation of innocence that materially aggravates their deliberate offence.

But Madame Ronner, through her long experience, has evolved a way to get them to pose as models. Her plan is the simple one of keeping her models prisoners in a glass box, enclosed in a wire cage, while she is painting them. Inside the prison she cannot always command their actions, but her knowledge of cat character enables her to a certain extent to persuade them to take the pose which she requires. By placing a comfortable cushion in the cage she can tempt her model to lie down; some object of great interest, like a live mouse, for instance, exhibited just outside the cage is sure to create the eager look that she has shown so well on cat faces; and to induce her kittens to indulge in the leaps and bounds which she has succeeded so wonderfully in transferring to canvas, she keeps hanging from the top of the cage a most seductive "bob."

Madame Ronner's favorite models are "Jem" and "Monmouth," cats of rare sweetness of temper, whose conduct in all relations of life is above reproach. The name of "Monmouth," as many will recall, was made famous by the hero of Monsieur La Bedolierre's classic, "Mother Michel and her Cat,"[2] and therefore has clustering about it traditions so glorious that its wearers in modern times must be upheld always by lofty hopes and high resolves. Doubtless Monmouth Ronner feels the responsibility entailed upon him by his name.

In the European galleries are several noted paintings in which the cat appears more or less unsuccessfully. Breughel and Teniers made their grotesque "Cat Concerts" famous, but one can scarcely see why, since the drawing is poor and there is no real insight into cat character evident. The sleeping cat, in Breughel's "Paradise Lost" in the Louvre, is better, being well drawn, but so small as to leave no chance for expression. Lebrun's "Sleep of the Infant Jesus," in the Louvre, has a slumbering cat under the stove, and in Barocci's "La Madonna del Gatto" the cat is the centre of interest. Holman Hunt's "The Awakening Conscience" and Murillo's Holy Family

---

2   Translated into English by Thomas Bailey Aldrich.

"del Pajarito" give the cat as a type of cruelty, but have failed egregiously in accuracy of form or expression. Paul Veronese's cat in "The Marriage at Cana" is fearfully and wonderfully made, and even Rembrandt failed when he tried to introduce a cat into his pictures.

Rosa Bonheur has been wise enough not to attempt cat pictures, knowing that special study, for which she had not the time or the inclination, is necessary to fit an artist to excel with the feline character. Landseer, too, after trying twice, once in 1819 with "The Cat Disturbed" and once in 1824 with "The Cat's Paw," gave up all attempts at dealing with Grimalkin. Indeed, most artists who have attempted it, have found that to be a wholly successful cat artist such whole-hearted devotion to the subject as Madame Ronner's is the invariable price of distinction.

Of late, however, more artists are found who are willing to pay this price, who are giving time and study not only to the subtle shadings of the delicate fur, but to the varying facial expression and sinuous movements of the cat. Margaret Stocks, of Munich, for example, is rapidly coming to the front as a cat painter, and some predict for her (she is still a young woman) a future equal to Madame Ronner's. Gambier Bolton's "Day Dreams" shows admirably the quality and "tumbled-ness" of an Angora kitten's fur, while the expression and drawing are equally good. Miss Cecilia Beaux's "Brighton Cats" is famous, and every student of cats recognizes its truthfulness at once.

Angora and Persian kittens find another loving and faithful student in J. Adam, whose paintings have been photographed and reproduced in this country times without number. "Puss in Boots" is another foreign picture which has been photographed and sold extensively in this country. "Little Milksop" by the same artist, Mr. Frank Paton, gives fairly faithful drawing and expression of two kittens who have broken a milk pitcher and are eagerly lapping up the contents.

In the Munich Gallery there is a painting by Claus Meyer, "Bose Zungen," which has become quite noted. His three old cats and three young cats show three gossiping old crones by the side of whom are three small and awkward kittens.

Of course, there are no artists whose painting of the cat is to be compared with Madame Ronner's. Mr. J.L. Dolph, of New York City, has painted hundreds of cat pieces which have found a ready sale, and Mr. Sid L. Brackett, of Boston, is doing very creditable work. A successful cat painter of the younger school is Mr. N.N.

Bickford, of New York, whose "Peek-a-Boo" hangs in a Chicago gallery side by side with cats of Madame Ronner and Monsieur Lambert. "Miss Kitty's Birthday" shows that he has genuine understanding of cat character, and is mastering the subtleties of long white fur.

Mr. Bickford is a pupil of Jules Lefebvre Boulanger and Miralles. It was by chance that he became a painter of cats. Mademoiselle Marie Engle, the prima-donna, owned a beautiful white Angora cat which she prized very highly, and as her engagements abroad compelled her to part with the cat for a short time, she left Mizzi with the artist until her return. One day Mr. Bickford thought he would try painting the white, silken fur of Mizzi: the result not only surprised him but also his artist friends, who said, "Lambert himself could not have done better."

Upon Miss Engle's return, seeing what an inspiration her cat had been, she gave her to Mr. Bickford, and it is needless to add that he has become deeply attached to his beautiful model. Mizzi is a pure white Angora, with beautiful blue eyes, and silky fur. She won first prize at the National Cat Show of 1895, but no longer attends cat shows, on account of her engagements as professional model.

Ben Austrian, who has made a success in painting other animals, has done a cat picture of considerable merit. The subject was Tix, a beautiful tiger-gray, belonging to Mr. Mahlon W. Newton, of Philadelphia. The cat is noted, not only in Philadel-phia, but among travelling men, as he resides at a hotel, and is quite a prominent member of the office force. He weighs fifteen pounds and is of a very affectionate nature, following his master to the park and about the establishment like a dog. During the day he lives in the office, lying on the counter or the key-rack, but at night he retires with his master at eleven or twelve o'clock, sleeping in his own bas-ket in the bathroom, and waking his master promptly at seven every morning. Tix's picture hangs in the office of his hotel, and is becoming as famous as the cat.

Elizabeth Bonsall is a young American artist who has exhibited some good cat pictures, and whose work promises to make her famous some day, if she does not "weary in well-doing"; and Mr. Jean Paul Selinger's "Kittens" are quite well known.

The good cat illustrator is even more rare than the cat painters. Thousands of readers recall those wonderfully lifelike cats and kittens which were a feature of the *St. Nicholas* a few years ago, accompanied by "nonsense rhymes" or "jingles."

They were the work of Joseph G. Francis, of Brookline, Mass., and brought him no little fame. He was, and is still, a broker on State Street, Boston, and in his busy life these inimitable cat sketches were but an incident. Mr. Francis is a devoted admirer of all cats, and had for many years loved and studied one cat in particular. It was by accident that he discovered his own possibilities in the line of cat drawing, as he began making little pen-and-ink sketches for his own amusement and then for that of his friends. The latter persuaded him to send some of these drawings to the *St. Nicholas* and the *Wide-Awake* magazines, and, rather to his surprise, they were promptly accepted, and the "Francis cats" became famous. Mr. Francis does but little artistic work, nowadays, more important business keeping him well occupied; besides, he says, he "is not in the mood for it."

Who does not know Louis Wain's cats?--that prince of English illustrators. Mr. Wain's home, when not in London, is at Bendigo Lodge, Westgate, Kent. He began his artistic career at nineteen, after a training in the best London schools. He was not a hard worker over his books, but his fondness for nature led him to an artist's career. American Indian stories were his delight, and accounts of the wandering outdoor life of our aborigines were instrumental in developing his powers of observation regarding the details of nature. Always fond of dumb animals, he began life by making sketches for sporting papers at agricultural shows all over England. It was his own cat "Peter" who first suggested to Louis Wain the fanciful cat creations which have made his name famous. Watching Peter's antics one evening, he was tempted to do a small study of kittens, which was promptly accepted by a magazine editor in London. Then he trained Peter to become a model and the starting-point of his success. Peter has done more to wipe out of England the contempt in which the cat was formerly held there, than any other feline in the world. He has done his race a service in raising their status from neglected, forlorn creatures on the one hand, or the pampered, overfed object of old maids' affections on the other, to a dignified place in the English house.

The double-page picture of the "Cat's Christmas Dance" in the *London Illustrated News* of December 6, 1890, contains a hundred and fifty cats, with as many varying facial expressions and attitudes. It occupied eleven working days of Mr. Wain's time, but it caught the public fancy and made a tremendous hit all over the world. Louis Wain's cats immediately became famous, and he has had more orders than he can fill ever since. He works eight hours a day, and then lays aside his brush to study physical science, or write a humorous story. He has written and illustrated a comic book, and spent a great deal of time over a more serious one.

Among the best known of his cat pictures, after the "Christmas Party," is his "Cats' Rights Meeting," which not even the most ardent suffragist can study without laughter. From a desk an ardent tabby is expounding, loud and long, on the rights of her kind. In front of her is a double row of felines, sitting with folded arms, and listening with absorbed attention. The expressions of these cats' faces, some ardent, some indignant, some placid, but all interested, form a ridiculous contrast to a row of "Toms" in the rear, who evidently disagree with the lecturer, and are prepared to hiss at her more "advanced" ideas. "Returning Thanks" is nearly as amusing, with its thirteen cats seated at table over their wine, while one offers thanks, and the remainder wear varying expressions of devotion, indifference, or irreverence. "Bringing Home the Yule Log" gives twenty-one cats, and as many individual expressions of joy or discomfort; and the "Snowball Match" shows a scene almost as hilarious as the "Christmas Dance."

Mr. Wain believes there is a great future for black and white work if a man is careful to keep abreast of the times. "A man should first of all create his public and draw upon his own fund of originality to sustain it," he says, "taking care not to pander to the degenerate tendencies which would prevent his work from elevating the finer instincts of the people." Says a recent visitor to the Wain household: "I wonder if Peter realizes that he has done more good than most human beings, who are endowed not only with sense but with brains? if in the firelight, he sees the faces of many a suffering child whose hours of pain have been shortened by the recital of his tricks, and the pictures of himself arrayed in white cravat, or gayly disporting himself on a 'see-saw'? I feel inclined to wake him up, and whisper how, one cold winter's night, I met a party of five little children, hatless and bootless, hurrying along an East-end slum, and saying encouragingly to the youngest, who was crying with cold and hunger, 'Come along: we'll get there soon.' I followed them down the lighted street till they paused in front of a barber's shop, and I heard their voices change to a shout of merriment: for in the window was a crumpled Christmas supplement, and Peter, in a frolicsome mood, was represented entertaining at a large cats' tea-party. Hunger, and cold, and misery were all dispelled. Who would not be a cat of Louis Wain's, capable of creating ten minutes' sunshine in a childish heart?"

Mr. Wain announces a discovery in relation to cats which corroborates a theory of my own, adopted from long observation and experience.

"I have found," he says, "as a result of many years of inquiry and study, that people who keep cats and are in the habit of petting them, do not suffer from those petty ailments which all flesh is heir to. Rheumatism and nervous complaints are uncommon with them, and Pussy's lovers are of the sweetest temperament. I have often felt the benefit, after a long spell of mental effort, of having my cats sitting across my shoulders, or of half an hour's chat with Peter."

This is a frequent experience of my own. Nothing is more restful and soothing after a busy day than sitting with my hands buried in the soft sides of one of my cats.

"Do you know," said one of my neighbors, recently, "when I am troubled with insomnia, lately, I get up and get Bingo from his bed, and take him to mine. I can go to sleep with my hands on him."

There is a powerful magnetic influence which emanates from a sleepy or even a quiet cat, that many an invalid has experienced without realizing it. If physicians were to investigate this feature of the cat's electrical and magnetic influence, in place of anatomical research after death, or the horrible practice of vivisection, they might be doing a real service to humanity.

Mr. Wain's success as an illustrator brought him great prominence in the National Cat Club of England, and he has been for a number of years its president, doing much to raise the condition and quality of cats and the status of the club. He has a number of beautiful and high-bred cats at Bendigo Lodge.

With regard to the painting of cats Champfleury said, "The lines are so delicate, the eyes are distinguished by such remarkable qualities, the movements are due to such sudden impulses, that to succeed in the portrayal of such a subject, one must be feline one's self." And Mr. Spielman gives the following advice to those who would paint cats:--

"You must love them, as Mahomet and Chesterfield loved them: be as fond of their company as Wolsley and Richelieu, Mazarin and Colbert, who retained them even during their most impressive audiences: as Petrarch, and Dr. Johnson, and

Canon Liddon, and Ludovic Halevy, who wrote with them at their elbow: and Tasso and Gray, who celebrated them in verse: as sympathetic as Carlyle, whom Mrs. Allingham painted in the company of his beloved 'Tib' in the garden at Chelsea, or as Whittington, the hero of our milk-and-water days: think of El Daher Beybars, who fed all feline comers, or 'La Belle Stewart,' Duchess of Richmond, who, in the words of the poet, 'endowed a college' for her little friends: you must be as approbative of their character, their amenableness to education, their inconstancy, not to say indifference and their general lack of principle, as Madame de Custine: and as appreciative of their daintiness and grace as Alfred de Musset. Then, and not till then, can you consider yourself sentimentally equipped for studying the art of cat painting."

CHAPTER XI
CONCERNING CAT HOSPITALS AND REFUGES

At comparatively frequent intervals we read of some woman, historic or modern, who has left an annuity (as the Duchess of Richmond, "La Belle Stewart") for the care of her pet cats; now and then a man provides for them in his will, as Lord Chesterfield, for instance, who left a permanent pension for his cats and their descendants. But I find only one who has endowed a home for them and given it sufficient means to support the strays and waifs who reach its shelter.

Early in the eighties, Captain Nathan Appleton, of Boston (a brother of the poet Longfellow's wife, and of Thomas Appleton, the celebrated wit), returned from a stay in London with a new idea, that of founding some sort of a refuge, or hospital, for sick or stray cats and dogs. He had visited Battersea, and been deeply impressed with the need of a shelter for small and friendless domestic animals.

At Battersea there is an institution similar to the one the Society for Prevention of Cruelty to Animals in New York have at East 120th Street, where stray animals may be sent and kept for a few days awaiting the possible appearance of a claimant or owner; at the end of which time the animals are placed in the "lethal chamber," where they die instantly and painlessly by asphyxiation. In Boston, the Society of Prevention of Cruelty to Animals have no such refuge or pound, but in place of it keep one or two men whose business it is to go wherever sent and "mercifully put to death" the superfluous, maimed, or sick animals that shall be given them.

Captain Appleton's idea, however, was something entirely different from this. These creatures, he argued, have a right to their lives and the pursuit of happiness after their own fashion, and he proposed to help them to enjoy that right. He appealed to a few sympathetic friends and gave two or three acres of land from his own estate, near "Nonantum Hill," where the Apostle Eliot preached to the Indians, and where his iodine springs are located. He had raised a thousand or two dollars and planned a structure of some kind to shelter stray dogs and cats, when the good angel that attends our household pets guided him to the lawyer who had charge of the estates of Miss Ellen M. Gifford, of New Haven, Ct. "I think I can help you," said the lawyer. But he would say nothing more at that time. A few weeks later, Captain Appleton was sent for. Miss Gifford had become deeply interested in the project, and after making more inquiries, gave the proposed home some twenty-five thousand dollars, adding to this amount afterward and providing for the institution in her will. It has already had over one hundred thousand dollars from Miss Gifford's estates, and it is so well endowed and well managed that it is self-supporting.

The Ellen M. Gifford Sheltering Home for Animals is situated near the Brookline edge of the Brighton district in Boston. In fact, the residential portion of aristocratic Brookline is so fast creeping up to it that the whole six acres of the institution will doubtless soon be disposed of at a very handsome profit, while the dogs and cats will retire to a more remote district to "live on the interest of their money."

The main building is a small but handsome brick affair, facing on Lake Street. This is the home of the superintendent, and contains, besides, the offices of the establishment. Over the office is a tablet with this inscription, taken from a letter of Miss Gifford's about the time the home was opened:--

"If only the waifs, the strays, the sick, the abused, would be sure to get entrance to the home, and anybody could feel at liberty to bring in a starved or ill-treated animal and have it cared for without pay, my object would be obtained. March 27, 1884."

The superintendent is a lover of animals as well as a good business manager, and his work is in line with the sentence just quoted. Any one wanting a cat or a dog, and who can promise it a good home, may apply there. But Mr. Perkins does not take the word of a stranger at random. He investigates their circumstances and character, and never gives away an animal unless he can be reasonably sure of its going to a good home. For instance, he once received an application from one man for six cats. The wholesale element in the order made him slightly suspicious, and he immediately drove to Boston, where he found that his would-be customer owned a big granary overrun with mice. He sent the six cats, and two weeks later went to see how they were getting on, when he found them living happily in a big grain-loft, fat and contented as the most devoted Sultan of Egypt could have asked. None but street cats and stray dogs, homeless waifs, ill-treated and half starved, are received at this home. Occasionally, some family desiring to get rid of the animal they have petted for months, perhaps years, will send it over to the Sheltering Home. But if Mr. Perkins can find where it came from he promptly returns it, for even this place, capable of comfortably housing a hundred cats and as many dogs, cannot accommodate all the unfortunates that are picked up in the streets of Boston. The accommodations, too, while they are comfortable and even luxurious for the poor creatures that have hitherto slept on ash-barrels and stone flaggings, are unfit for household pets that have slept on cushions, soft rugs, and milady's bed.

There is a dog-house and a cat-house, sufficiently far apart that the occupants of one need not be disturbed by those of the other. In the dog-house there are rows of pens on each side of the middle aisle, in which from one to four or five dogs, according to size, are kept when indoors. These are of all sorts, colors, dispositions, and sizes, ranging from pugs to St. Bernards, terriers to mastiffs. There are few purely bred dogs, although there are many intelligent and really handsome ones. The dogs are allowed to run in the big yard that opens out from their house at certain hours of the day; but the cats' yards are open to them all day and night. All yards and runs are enclosed with wire netting, and the cat-house has partitions of the same. All around the sides of the cat-house are shelves or bunks, which are kept supplied with clean hay, for their beds. Here one may see cats of every color and assorted sizes, contentedly curled up in their nests, while their companions sit blinking in the sun, or run out in the yards. Cooked meat, crackers and milk, and dishes of fresh water are kept where they can get at them. The cats all look plump and well fed, and, indeed, the ordinary street cat must feel that his lines have fallen in pleasant places.

Not so, however, with pet cats who may be housed there. They miss the companionship of people, and the household belongings to which they have been accustomed. Sometimes it is really pathetic to see one of these cast-off pets climb up the wire netting and plainly beg the visitor to take him away from that strange place, and give him such a home as he has been used to. In the superintendent's house there is usually a good cat or two of this sort, as he is apt to test a well-bred cat before giving him away.

Somewhat similar, and even older than the Ellen Gifford Sheltering Home, is the Morris Refuge of Philadelphia. This institution, whose motto is "The Lord is good to all: and his tender mercies are over all his works," was first established in May, 1874, by Miss Elizabeth Morris and other ladies who took an interest in the protection of suffering animals. It does not limit its tender mercies to cats and dogs, but cares for every suffering animal. It differs from the Ellen Gifford Home chiefly in the fact that, while the latter is a *home* for stray cats and dogs, the Morris Refuge has for its object the care for and disposal of suffering animals of all sorts. In a word, it brings relief to most of these unfortunate creatures by means of a swift and pain-less death.

It was first known as the City Refuge, although it was never maintained by the city. In January, 1889, it was reorganized and incorporated as the "Morris Refuge for Homeless and Suffering Animals." It is supported by private contributions, and is under the supervision of Miss Morris and a corps of kind-hearted ladies of Phila-delphia. A wagon is kept at the home to respond to calls, and visits any residence where suffering animals may need attention. The agent of the society lives at the refuge with his family, and receives animals at any time. When notice is received of an animal hurt or suffering, he sends after it. Chloroform is invariably taken along, in order that, if expedient, the creature may be put out of its agony at once. This refuge is at 1242 Lombard Street, and there is a temporary home where dogs are boarded at 923 South 11th Street.

In 1895, out of 23,067 animals coming under the care of the association, 19,672 were cats. In 1896, there were 24,037 animals relieved and disposed of, while the superintendent answered 230 police calls. Good homes are found for both dogs and cats, but not until the agent is sure that they will be kindly treated.

In Miss Morris's eighth annual report she says: "Looking back to the formation of the first society for the prevention of cruelty to animals, we find since that time a gradual awakening to the duties man owes to those below him in the scale of animal creation. The titles of those societies and their objects, as defined by their charters, show that at first it was considered sufficient to protect animals from cruel treat-ment: very few people gave thought to the care of those that were without homes. Now many are beginning to think of the evil of being overrun with numbers of homeless creatures, whose sufferings appeal to the sympathies of the humane, and whose noise and depredations provoke the cruelty of the hard-hearted: hence the efforts that are being made in different cities to establish refuges. A request has lately been received from Montreal asking for our reports, as it is proposed to found a home for animals in that city, and information is being collected in relation to such institutions."

Lady Marcus Beresford has succeeded in establishing and endowing a home for cats in Englefield Green, Windsor Park. She has made a specialty of Angoras, and her collection is famous. Queen Victoria and her daughters take a deep interest, not alone in finely bred cats, but in poor and homeless waifs as well. Her Royal Highness, in fact, took pains to write the London S.P.C.A. some years ago, saying she would be very glad to have them do something for the safety and protection of cats, "which are so generally misunderstood and grossly ill-treated." She herself sets a good example in this respect, and when her courts remove from one royal residence to another, her cats are taken with her.

There is a movement in Paris, too, to provide for sick and homeless cats as well as dogs. Two English ladies have founded a hospital near Asnieres, where ailing pets can be tended in illness, or boarded for about ten cents a day; and very well cared for their pensioners are. There is also a charity ward where pauper patients are received and tended carefully, and afterward sold or given away to reliable people. Oddly, this sort of charity was begun by Mademoiselle Claude Bernard, the daughter of the great scientist who, it is said, tortured more living creatures to death than any other. Vivisection became a passion with him, but Mademoiselle Bernard is atoning for her father's cruelty by a singular devotion to animals, and none are turned from her gates.

This is the way they do it in Cairo even now, according to Monsieur Prisse d'Avennes, the distinguished Egyptologist:--

"The Sultan, El Daher Beybars, who reigned in Egypt and Syria toward 658 of the Hegira (1260 A.D.) and is compared by William of Tripoli to Nero in wickedness, and to Caesar in bravery, had a peculiar affection for cats. At his death, he left a garden, 'Gheyt-el-Quoltah' (the cats' orchard), situated near his mosque outside Cairo, for the support of homeless cats. Subsequently the field was sold and resold several times by the administrator and purchasers. In consequence of a series of dilapidations it now produces a nominal rent of fifteen piastres a year, which with certain other legacies is appropriated to the maintenance of cats. The Kadi, who is the official administrator of all pious and charitable bequests, ordains that at the hour of afternoon prayer, between noon and sunset, a daily distribution of animals' entrails and refuse meat from the butchers' stalls, chopped up together, shall be made to the cats of the neighborhood. This takes place in the outer court of the 'Mehkemeh,' or tribunal, and a curious spectacle may then be seen. At this hour all the terraces near the Mehkemeh are crowded with cats: they come jumping from house to house across the narrow Cairo streets, hurrying for their share: they slide down walls and glide into the court, where they dispute, with great tenacity and much growling, the scanty meal so sadly out of proportion to the number of guests. The old ones clear the food in a moment: the young ones and the newcomers, too timid to fight for their chance, must content themselves with licking the ground. Those wanting to get rid of cats take them there and deposit them. I have seen whole baskets of kittens deposited in the court, greatly to the annoyance of the neighbors."

There are similar customs in Italy and Switzerland. In Geneva cats prowl about the streets like dogs at Constantinople. The people charge themselves with their maintenance, and feed the cats who come to their doors at the same hour every day for their meals.

In Florence, a cloister near St. Lorenzo's Church serves as a refuge for cats. It is an ancient and curious institution, but I am unable to find whether it is maintained by the city or by private charities. There are specimens of all colors, sizes, and kinds, and any one who wants a cat has but to go there and ask for it. On the other hand, the owner of a cat who is unable or unwilling to keep it may take it there, where it is fed and well treated.

In Rome, they have a commendable system of caring for their cats. At a certain hour butchers' men drive through the city, with carts well stocked with cat's meat. They utter a peculiar cry which the cats recognize, and come hurrying out of the houses for their allowances, which are paid for by the owners at a certain rate per month.

In Boston, during the summer of 1895, a firm of butchers took subscriptions from philanthropic citizens, and raised enough to defray the expenses of feeding the cats on the Back Bay,--where, in spite of the fact that the citizens are all wealthy and supposedly humane, there are more starving cats than elsewhere in the city. But the experiment has not been repeated.

Hospitals for sick animals are no new thing, but a really comfortable home for cats is an enterprise in which many a woman who now asks despondently what she can do in this overcrowded world to earn a living, might find pleasant and profitable.

A most worthy charity is that of the Animal Rescue League in Boston, which was started by Mrs. Anna Harris Smith in 1899. She put a call in the newspapers, asking those who were interested in the subject to attend a meeting and form a league for the protection and care of lost or deserted pets. The response was immediate and generous. The Animal Rescue League was formed with several hundred members, and in a short time the house at 68 Carver Street was rented, and a man and his wife put in charge. Here are brought both cats and dogs from all parts of Boston and the suburbs, where they are sure of kind treatment and care. If they are diseased they are immediately put out of existence by means of the lethal chamber; otherwise they are kept for a few days in order that they may be claimed by their owners if lost, or have homes found for them whenever it is possible. During the first year over two thousand cats were cared for, and several hundred dogs. This home is maintained by voluntary contributions and by the annual dues of subscribers. These are one dollar a year for associate members and five dollars for active members. It is an excellent charity, and one that may well be emulated in other cities.

There are several cat asylums and refuges in the Far West, and certainly a few more such institutions as the Sheltering Home at Brighton, Mass., or the Morris Refuge would be a credit to a country. How better than by applying it to our cats can we demonstrate the truth of Solomon's maxim, "A merciful man is merciful to his beast"?

CHAPTER XII
CONCERNING THE ORIGIN OF CATS

I f any of my readers hunger and thirst for information concerning the descent of the cat through marsupial ancestors and mesozoic mammals to the generalized placental or monodelphous carnivora of to-day, let them consult St. George Mivart, who gives altogether the most comprehensive and exhaustive scientific study to the cat ever published, and whose book on the cat is an excellent work for the earnest beginner in the study of biological science. He says no more complete example can be found of a perfectly organized living being than that supplied by the highest mammalian family--Felidae.

"On the whole," he sums up, "it seems probable that the mammalia, and therefore the cat, descends from some highly developed, somewhat reptile-like batrachian of which no trace has been found."

Away back in the eighth century of the Hegira, an Arab naturalist gives this account of the creation of the cat: "When, as the Arab relates, Noah made a couple of each animal to enter the ark, his companions and family asked, 'What security can you give us and the other animals, so long as the lion dwells with us on this narrow vessel?' Then Noah betook himself to prayer, and entreated the Lord God. Immediately fever came down from heaven and seized upon the king of beasts." This was the origin of fever. But constituents in Noah's time, as now, were ungrateful; and no sooner was the lion disposed of, than the mouse was discovered to be an object of suspicion. They complained that there would be no safety for provisions or clothing. "And so Noah renewed his supplication to the Most High, the lion sneezed, and a cat ran out of his nostrils. From that time the mouse has been timid and has hidden in holes."

In the Egyptian gallery of the British Museum there is an excellent painting of a tabby cat assisting a man to capture birds. Hieroglyphic inscriptions as far back as 1684 B.C. mention the cat, and there is at Leyden a tablet of the eighteenth or nineteenth dynasty with a cat seated under a chair. A temple at Beni-Hassan is dedicated to Pasht or Bubastis, the goddess of cats, which is as old as Thothmes IV of the eighteenth dynasty, 1500 B.C.; and the cat appears in written rituals of that dynasty. Herodotus tells of the almost superstitious reverence which dwellers along the Nile felt for the cat, and gravely states that when one died a natural death in any house, the inmates shaved their eyebrows as a token of grief; also, that in case of a fire the first thing they saved was the household cat. Fortunate pussies!

It is thought that cats were introduced into Greece from Egypt, although Professor Rolleston, of Cambridge University, believes the Grecian pet cat to have been the white-breasted marten. Yet why should he? Is not a soft, white-breasted maltese or tabby as attractive? The idea that cats were domesticated in Western Europe by the Crusaders is thought to be erroneous; but pet cats were often found in nunneries in the Middle Ages, and Pope Gregory the Great, toward the end of the sixth century, had a pet cat of which he was very fond.

An old writer says, "A favorite cat sometimes accompanied the Egyptians on these occasions [of sport], and the artist of that day intends to show us by the exactness with which he represents her seizing her prey, that cats were trained to hunt and carry water-fowl." There are old Egyptian paintings representing sporting scenes along the Nile, where the cats plunge into the water of the marshes to retrieve and carry game; while plenty of mural paintings show them sitting under the arm-chair of the mistress of the house. Modern naturalists, however, claim a radical difference between those old Egyptian retrieving cats and our water-hating pussies. There are no records of cats between that period in Egypt, about 1630 B.C., and 260 B.C., when they seem to have become acclimated in Greece and Rome. There is in the Bordeaux Museum an ancient picture of a young girl holding a cat, on a tomb of the Gallo-Roman Epoch, and cats appeared in the heraldry of that date; but writers of those ages speak rather slightingly of them. Then for centuries the cat was looked upon as a diabolic creature, fit company for witches.

"Why," says Balthazar Bekker in the seventeenth century, "is a cat always found among the belongings of witches, when according to the Sacred Book, and Apocalypse in particular, it is the dog, not a feline animal, that consorts with the sorcerers?"

In Russia even yet the common people believe that black cats become devils at the end of seven years, and in many parts of Southern Europe they are still supposed to be serving apprenticeship as witches. In Sicily the peasants are sure that if a black cat lives with seven masters, the soul of the seventh will surely accompany him back to the dominion of Hades. In Brittany there is a dreadful tale of cats that dance with unholy glee around the crucifix while their King is being put to death. Cats figure in Norwegian folk-lore, too, as witches and picturesque incumbents of ghost-haunted houses and nocturnal revels. And even to-day there is a legend in Westminster to the effect that the dissipated cats of that region indulge in a most disreputable revel in some country house, and that is why they look so forlorn and altogether undone by daylight.

A canon enacted in England in 1127 forbade any abbess or nun to use more costly fur than that of lambs or cats, and it is proved that cat-fur was at that time commonly used for trimming dresses. The cat was, probably for that reason, an object of chase in royal forests, and a license is still in existence from Richard II to the Abbot of Peterborough, and dated 1239, granting liberty to hunt cats. This was probably the wild cat, however, which was not the same as the domestic.[3]

---

3   These are among the laws supposedly enacted by Hoel Dha (Howell the Good) sometime between 915 and 948 A.D.

The Vendotian Code XI.

The worth of a cat and her teithi (qualities) this is:--

1st. The worth of a kitten from the night it is kittened until it shall open its eyes, is one penny.

2d. And from that time until it shall kill mice, two pence.

3d. And after it shall kill mice, four legal pence; and so it shall always remain.

4th. Her teithe are to see, to hear, to kill mice, and to have her claws.

This is the "Dimentian Code." XXXII. Of Cats.

1st. The worth of a cat that is killed or stolen. Its head to be put downward upon a clean, even floor, with its tail lifted upward and thus suspended, whilst wheat is poured about it until the top of its tail be covered and that is to be its worth. If the corn cannot be had, then a milch sheep with a lamb and its wool is its value, if it be a cat that guards the king's barn.

2d. The worth of a common cat is four legal pence.

3d. The teithi of a cat, and of every animal upon the milk of which people do not feed, is the third part of its worth or the worth of its litter.

4th. Whosoever shall sell a cat (cath) is to answer that she devour not her kittens, and that she

That cats, even in the Middle Ages, were thought much more highly of in Great Britain than on the Continent is proved by the fact that the laws there imposed a heavy fine on cat-killers, the fine being as much wheat as would serve to bury the cat when he was held up by the tip of the tail with his nose on the ground. So that pet cats stood a fairly good chance in those days.

One of the good things remembered of Louis XIII is that he interceded as Dauphin with Henri IV for the lives of the cats about to be burned at the festival on St. John's Day.

Nowadays, there is a current superstition that a black cat brings good luck to a house; but in the Middle Ages they believed that the devil borrowed the form of a black cat when he wanted to torment or get control of his victims. There are plenty of old traditions about cats having spoken to human beings, and been kicked, or struck, or burned by them in return; and invariably, these tales tell us, those who are so bespoken meet some one the next day with plain marks of the injury they had inflicted on the froward cat,--which was sure evidence of witchery and sorcery. Doubtless full many a human being has been put to death, in times past, on no stronger evidence of being a witch. Humanity did not come to the rescue of the cat and bring her out from the shadow of ignominy that hung over her in mediaeval

---

have ears, teeth, eyes, and nails, and be a good mouser.

The "Gwentian Code" begins in the same way, but says:--

3d. That it be perfect of ear, perfect of eye, perfect of teeth, perfect of tail, perfect of claw, and without marks of fire. And if the cat fall short in any of these particulars, a third of her price had to be refunded. As to the fire, in case her fur had been singed the rats could detect her by the odor, and her qualities as a mouser were thus injured. And then it goes on to say:--

4th. That the teithi and the legal worth of a cat are coequal.

5th. A pound is the worth of a pet animal of the king.

6th. The pet animal of a breyer (brewer) is six score pence in value.

7th. The pet animal of a taoog is a curt penny in value.

In the 39th chapter, 53d section, we find that "there are three animals whose tails, eyes, and lives are of the same value--a calf, a filly for common work, and a cat, except the cat which shall watch the king's barn," in which case she was more valuable.

Another old Welsh law says: "Three animals reach their worth in a year: a sheep, a cat, and a cur. This is a complement of the legal hamlet; nine buildings, one plough, one kiln, one churn, and one cat, one cock, one bull, and one herdsman."

In order that there might be no mistake in regard to the cat, a rough sketch of Puss is given in the Mss. of the laws.

times until 1618, when an interdict was issued in Flanders prohibiting the festive ceremony of throwing cats from the high tower of Ypres on Wednesdays of the second week in Lent. And from that time Pussy's fortunes began to look up.

To-day, travellers on the edge of the Pyrenees know a little old man, Martre Tolosan, who makes and sells replicas of the original models of cats found among the Roman remains at a small town near Toulouse. These are made in blue and white earthenware and each one is numbered. Mine, bought by a friend in 1895, is marked 5000. They are not exact models of our cats of to-day, to be sure, but they express all the snug content and inscrutable calm of our modern pets.

The Chinese reproduce cats in their ceramics in white, turquoise blue, and old violet. One that once belonged to Madame de Mazarin sold for eight hundred livres. In Japan, cats are reproduced in common ware, daubed with paint, but the Chinese make them of finer ware, enamelling the commoner kinds of porcelain and using the cat in conventional forms as flower-vases and lamps.

CHAPTER XIII
CONCERNING VARIETIES OF CATS

Few people realize how many kinds of cats there are. The fashionable world begins to discuss cats technically and understand their various points of excellence. The "lord mayor's chain," the "Dutch rabbit markings," and similar features are understood by more cat fanciers than a few years ago; but, until within that time, it is doubtful if the number of people who knew the difference between the Angora and the Persian in this country amounted to a hundred. It is but a few years since the craze for the Angora cat started. These cats have been fashionable pets in England for some years back, and now America begins to understand their value and the principles of breeding them. Today, there are as handsome, well-bred animals in the United States as can be found abroad. The demand for high-bred animals with a pedigree is greatly increasing, and society people are beginning to understand the fine points of the thoroughbred.

The Angora cat, as its name indicates, comes from Angora in Western Asia, the province that is celebrated for its goats with long hair of fine quality. In fact, the hair under the Angora cat's body often resembles the finest of the Angora goatskins. Angora cats are favorites with the Turks and Armenians, and exist in many colors, especially since they have been more carefully bred. They vary in form, color, and disposition, and also in the quality of their hair. The standard calls for a small head, with not too long a nose, large eyes that should harmonize in color with the fur, small, pointed ears with a tuft of hair at the apex, and a very full, fluffy mane around the neck. This mane is known as the "lord mayor's chain." The body is longer than that of the ordinary cat in proportion to its size, and is extremely graceful, and covered with long, silky hair, which is crinkly like that of the Angora goat. This hair should be as fine as possible, and not woolly. The legs are of a moderate length, but

look short on account of the length of hair on the body. Little tufts of hair growing between the toes indicate high breeding. The Angora cat, in good condition, is
one of the most beautiful and elegant creatures in the world, and few can resist its
charm. The tail is long and like an ostrich plume. It is usually carried, when the cat
is in good spirits, straight up, with the end waving over toward one side. The tail of
the Angora serves as a barometer of its bodily and mental condition. If the cat is ill
or frightened, the tail droops, and sometimes trails on the ground; but when she is
in good spirits, playing about the house or grounds, it waves like a great plume, and
is exceedingly handsome. The suppleness of the Angora's tail is also a mark of fine
breeding. A highbred Angora will allow its tail to be doubled or twisted without
apparent notice of the performance.

The Angora does not reach its prime until about two years. Before that time
its head and body are not sufficiently developed to give the full beauty and grace
of the animal. As a rule, the Angora is of good disposition, although the females are
apt to be exceedingly nervous. They are sociable and docile, although fond of roam-
ing about, especially if allowed to run loose. As a rule, they do not possess the keen
intelligence of the ordinary short-haired family cat, but their great beauty and their
cleanly and affectionate habits make them favorites with fashionable people. The
proper breeding of the Angora cat is a regular science. Of the colors of the Angoras,
the blue or maltese is a favorite, and rather common, especially when mixed with
white.

The white Angora is extraordinarily beautiful, and brings a high price when
it has blue eyes and all its points are equally good. The orange, or yellow, and the
black with amber eyes are also prize winners. There are the tigers also, the brown
tabby, and the orange and white. Mixed colors are more common than solid ones;
the tortoise-shell cat of three colors and well mottled being considered particularly
desirable.

The Persian cat differs from the Angora in the quality of its fur, although the
ordinary observer sees little difference between them. All the long-haired cats originated from the Indian Bengalese, Thibetan, and other wild cats of Asia and Russia. The Persian cat of very great value is all black, with a very fluffy frill, or lord
mayor's chain, and orange eyes. Next to him comes a light slate or blue Persian,
with yellow eyes. The fur of the Persian cat is much more woolly than that of the

Angora, and sometimes in hot weather mats badly. The difference between a Persian and an Angora can usually be told by an amateur, by drawing the tail between the thumb and first finger. The Angora's tail comes out thin, silky, and narrow, although it immediately "fluffs" up. The Persian's tail does not compress itself readily into a small space. The Persian cat's head is larger, its ears are less pointed, although it should have the tuft at the end and the long hair inside. It is usually larger in body and apparently stronger made, although slender and elegant in appearance, with small bones and graceful in movement. The colors vary, as with the Angora, except that the tortoise-shell and the dark-marked tabby do not so frequently appear. The temper is usually less reliable and the intelligence less keen than the Angora.

The Russian long-haired pet is much less common even than the Persian and Angora. It is fond of cold weather, and its fur is denser, indicating that it has been used to colder regions. Many of the cats that we see are crosses of Angora and Persian, or Angora and Russian, so that it is extremely difficult for the amateur to know a thoroughbred cat which has not been mixed with other varieties.

There is also a fine short-haired cat coming from Russia, usually self-colored. Mrs. Frederick Monroe, of Chicago, owns a very handsome blue and white one.

In Pegu, Siam, and Burmah, there is a race of cats known as the Malay cat, with tails only half the ordinary length and often contorted into a sort of a knot that cannot be straightened, after the fashion of the pug dog or ordinary pig.

There is another cat known as the Mombas, a native of the west coast of Africa and covered with stiff, bristling hair. Paraguay cats are only one-quarter as big as our ordinary cat, and are found along the western coast of South America, even as far north as Mexico.

The royal cat of Siam is a short-haired cat, yet widely different from other short-haired varieties. They are extremely pretty, with blue or amber-colored eyes by day which grow brilliant at night. These cats also frequently have the kink in the tail, and sometimes a strong animal odor, although this is not disagreeable. The head is rather longer than the ordinary cat's, tapering off sharply toward the muzzle, the forehead flat and receding, and the eyes more slanting toward the nose than the American cat's. The form should be slender, graceful, and delicately made; the body long; the tail very thin and rather short; the legs short and slender, and the feet oval. The body is of a bright, uniform color, and the legs, feet, and tail are usually black.

The Manx cat is considered by many people as a natural curiosity. It differs from the ordinary domestic cat but little, except in the absence of a tail, or even an apology for one. The hind legs are thicker and rather longer than the ordinary cat's, and it runs more like a hare. It is not a graceful object when seen from behind, but it is an affectionate, home-loving creature with considerable intelligence. The Manx cat came from the Isle of Man originally, and is a distinct breed. So-called Manx cats have tails from one to a few inches long, but these are crosses of the Manx and the ordinary cat. In the Crimea is found another kind of cat which has no tail. The cats known as the "celebrated orange cats of Venice," are probably descendants of the old Egyptian cat, and are of varying shades of yellow, sometimes deepening into a sandy color which is almost red. There are obscure stripes on the body, which become more distinct on the limbs. The tail is more or less ringed toward its termination.

There has been a newspaper paragraph floating about stating that a prize of several thousand dollars had been offered in England for a male tortoise-shell cat. This is probably not true, as a Mr. Smith exhibited a tortoise-shell he-cat at the Crystal Palace Show of 1871. Several tortoise-shell and white toms have been exhibited since, and one of these has taken nine first prizes at the Crystal Palace Show; but the tortoise-shell he-cat is extremely rare. The real tortoise-shell is not a striped tiger nor a tabby. It has three colors usually, black, yellow, and red or brown; but these appear in patches rather than stripes. It is said that the tortoise-shell cat is common in Egypt and the south of Europe. It comes from a different stock than the ordinary short-haired cat, the texture of the hair being different, as well as the color. The tortoise-shell and white cat is much more common, and is the product of a cross between a tortoise shell and a solid color cat. In this case the hair is usually coarser and the tail thicker than in the ordinary cat.

Among cat fanciers there is a distinctive variety known as the tortoise-shell tabby. As the tabby cat is one of the varieties of striped or spotted cats having markings, broad or narrow, of bands of black on a dark tan or gray ground, the tortoise-shell cat would have both stripes and patches of color.

Of the tabbies, there are brown tabbies, silver tabbies, and red tabbies. It is said that the red tabby she-cat is as scarce as the tortoise-shell he-cat. The ordinary observer considers the brown tabby with white markings as much the handsomest of the tabbies. But fanciers and judges do not agree with him, the cats having nar-row bands and spots being the ones to take prizes. The word "tabby," according to Harrison Weir, was derived from a kind of taffeta or ribbed silk which used to be called tabby silk. Other authorities state that tabby cats got their name from Atab, a street in Bagdad; but as this street was famous for its watered silks perhaps the same reason holds. The tortoise-shell used to be called, in England, the Calimanco. In America, it is sometimes called the calico cat.

The red tabby is of a deep reddish or yellow brown, with a well-ringed tail, orange or yellow eyes, and pink cushions to the feet. The brown tabby is orange brown, with black lips, brown whiskers, black feet, black pads, long tail, greenish orange eyes, and red nose bordered with black. The spotted tabby must have no bands at all. It must be brown, red, or yellow, with black spots. In the brown tabby the feet and pads are black; in the yellow and red, the feet and pads are pink. The spotted cat sometimes resembles a leopard, while the banded tabby resembles more the tiger. Some of the spotted tabbies are extremely handsome, and came originally from a cross between the ordinary cat and the wild cat.

"Self-colored cats" are entirely of one color, which may vary in different cats, but must never be mixed in the same cat, nor even shaded into a lighter tone on the animal; and whether this color be black, blue, red, or yellow, the self-colored cat should have a rich deep tint. Of course the short-haired white cat is the handsom-est of all. One of the peculiarities of this white cat is that it is apt to be deaf. The most valuable white cats, whether long or short haired, have blue eyes. Sometimes they have one blue eye and one green or yellow, which gives a comical effect, and detracts from their value. By the way, cross-eyed cats are not unknown. The best white cats have a yellowish white tint instead of grayish white, as the latter have a coarser quality of fur.

The jet-black cat is thought by many to be the most desirable. The true black cat should have a uniform, intensely black coat, velvety and extremely glossy; the eyes should be round and full, and of a brilliant amber; the nose and pads of the feet should be jet-black, and the tail long and tapering. It is difficult to find a black cat without a white hair, as usually there are a few under the chin or on the belly.

The blue cat is the one ordinarily known in this country as the dark maltese. There is a tradition that it came from the Island of Malta. Many people do not consider it a distinct breed, but think it a light-colored variety of the black cat. It is known sometimes as the Archangel, sometimes as the Russian blue, the Spanish blue, the Chartreuse blue, but more commonly in this country as the maltese. When it is of a deep bluish color, or of the soft silver-gray maltese without stripes, it is extremely handsome. The most desirable are the bluish lilac-colored ones, with soft fur like sealskin. The nose and pads of the feet are dark, and the eyes are orange yellow. The maltese and white cat when well marked is extremely handsome, and there is no prettier kitten than the maltese and white.

The black and white, yellow and white, blue and white, and in fact, any self-colored and white cat is a mixture of the other breeds. If well marked they are extremely handsome and are usually bright and intelligent.

The solid gray cat is very rare. It is, in fact, a tabby without the black stripes or spots.

In Australia, New Zealand, and New Guinea there used to be no cat of any kind. The Siamese cat has been imported to Australia, and some authorities claim that the cats known in this country as Australian cats are of Siamese origin. Madagascar is a catless region.

There is in this country a variety known as the "coon cat," which is handsome, especially in the solid black. Its native home is in Maine, and it is thought by many to have originated with the ordinary cat and the raccoon. It grows somewhat larger than the ordinary cat, with thick, woolly fur and an extremely bushy tail. It is fond of outdoor life, and when kept as a pet must be allowed to run out of doors or it is apt to become so savage and disagreeable that nothing can be done with it. When it is allowed its freedom, however, it becomes affectionate, intelligent, and is usually a handsome cat.

The term "Dutch rabbit markings" refers to the white markings on the cat of two or three colors. Evidently, the cats themselves understand the value of Dutch rabbit markings, as one which has them is invariably proud of them. A cat that has white mittens, for instance, is often inordinately vain, and keeps them in the most immaculate state of cleanliness.

CHAPTER XIV
CONCERNING CAT LANGUAGE

Montaigne it was who said: "We have some intelligence of their senses: so have also the beasts of ours in much the same measure. They flatter us, menace us, need us, and we them. It is manifestly evident that there is among them a full and entire communication, and that they understand each other."

That this applies to cats is certainly true. Did you ever notice how a mother cat talks to her children, and simply by the utterances of her voice induces them to abandon their play and go with her, sometimes with the greatest reluctance, to some place that suited her whim--or her wisdom?

Dupont de Nemours, a naturalist of the eighteenth century, made himself ridiculous in the eyes of his compatriots by seeking to penetrate the mysteries of animal language. "Those who utter sounds," he affirmed, "attach significance to them; their fellows do the same, and those sounds originally inspired by passion and repeated under similar recurrent circumstances, become the abiding expressions of the passions that gave rise to them."

Fortified by this theory he devoted a couple of years to the study of crow language, and made himself ridiculous in the eyes of his adversaries by attempting to translate a nightingale's song.

Chateaubriand was much interested in Dupont de Nemours's researches into the language of cats. "Its claws," says the latter, "and the power of climbing trees which its claws give it, furnish the cat with resources of experience and ideas denied the dog. The cat, also, has the advantage of a language which has the same vowels as pronounced by the dog, and with six consonants in addition, *m, n, g, h, v*, and *f*. Consequently the cat has a greater number of words. These two causes, the finer structure of its paws, and the larger scope of oral language, endow the solitary cat with greater cunning and skill as a hunter than the dog."

Abbe Galiani also says: "For centuries cats have been reared, but I do not find they have ever been really studied. I have a male and a female cat. I have cut them off from all communication with cats outside the house, and closely observe their proceedings. During their courtship they never once miowed: the miow, therefore, is not the language of love, but rather the call of the absent. Another positive discovery I have made is that the voice of the male is entirely different from that of the female, as it should be. I am sure there are more than twenty different inflections in the language of cats, and there is really a 'tongue' for they always employ the same sound to express the same thing."

I heartily concur with him, and in addition have often noticed the wide difference between the voice and manner of expression of the gelded cat and the ordinary tom. The former has a thin, high voice with much smaller vocabulary. As a rule, the gelded cat does not "mew" to make known his wants, but employs his voice for conversational purposes. A mother cat "talks" much more than any other, and more when she has small kittens than at other times.

Cat language has been reduced to etymology in several tongues. In Arabia their speech is called naoua; in Chinese, ming; in Greek, larungizein; in Sanscrit, madj, vid, bid; in German, miauen; in French miauler; and in English, mew or "mi-aouw."

Perhaps, if Professor Garner had turned his attention to cat language instead of monkeys we would know more about it. But a French professor, Alphonse Leon Grimaldi, of Paris, claims that cats can talk as readily as human beings, and that he has learned their language so as to be able to converse with them to some extent. Grimaldi goes even further: he not only says that he knows such a language, but he states definitely that there are about six hundred words in it, that it is more like modern Chinese than anything else, and to prove this contention, gives a small vocabulary.

Most of us would prefer to accept St. George Mivart's conclusions, that the difference between all animals and human beings is that while they have some means of communication, or language, we only have the gift of speech. Among the eighteen distinct active powers which he attributes to the cat, he quotes: "16th, powers of pleasurable or painful excitement on the occurrence of sense-perceptions with imaginations, **emotions**;" and "17th, a power of expressing feelings by sounds or gestures which may affect other individuals,--emotional language."

Again he says: "The cat has a language of sounds and gestures to express its feelings and emotions. So have we. But we have further--which neither the cat, nor the bird, nor the beast has--a language and gestures to express our thoughts." The sum of his conclusions seems to be that while the cat has a most highly developed nervous system, and much of what is known as "animal intelligence," it is not a human intelligence--not consciousness, but "con-sentience."

Elsewhere St. George Mivart doubts if a cat distinguishes odors as such. Perhaps a cat starts for the kitchen the instant he smells meat because of the mental association of the scent with the gratification of hunger; but why, pray tell, do some cats evince such delight in delicate perfumes? Our own Pomp the First, for instance, had a most demonstrative fondness for violets, and liked the scent of all flowers. One winter I used to bring home a bunch of Parma or Russian violets every day or two, and put them in a small glass bowl of water. It soon became necessary to put them on the highest shelf in the room, and even then Pompey would find them. Often have I placed them on the piano, and a few minutes later seen him enter the room, lift his nose, give a few sniffs, and then go straight to the piano, bury his nose in the violets, and hold it there in perfect ecstacy. And usually, wherever they were placed, the bunch was found the next morning on the floor, where Pompey had carried the violets, and holding them between his paws for a time, had surfeited himself with their delicious fragrance.

Still, I am not prepared to say that Pompey had any word for violets, or for anything else that ministered to his delight. It was enough for him to be happy; and he had better ways of expressing it.

Cats do have the power of making people understand what they want done, but so far as my knowledge of them goes, some of the most intelligent ones "talk" the least. Thomas Erastus, whose intelligence sometimes amounts to a knowledge that seems almost uncanny, seldom utters a sound.

There is--or was--a black cat belonging to the city jail of a Californian town, named "Inspector Byrnes," because of his remarkable assistance to the police force. When, one night, a prisoner in the jail had stuffed the cracks to his cell with straw, and turned on the gas in an attempt to commit suicide, "Inspector Byrnes" hurried off and notified the night keeper that something was wrong, and induced him to go to the cell in time to save the prisoner's life. He once notified the police when a fire broke out on the premises, and at another time made such a fuss that they followed him--to discover a woman trying to hang herself. Again, some of the prisoners plotted to escape, and the cat crawled through the hole they had filed and called the warden's attention to it. In fact, there was no doubt that "Inspector Byrnes" considered himself assistant warden at the jail, and he did not waste much time in talk either. The Pretty Lady had ways of her own to make us know when things were wrong in the household, although she used to utter a great many sounds, either of pleasure or perturbation, which we came to understand. I remember one morning, when my sister was ill upstairs, that I had breakfasted and sat down to read my morning's mail, when the Pretty Lady came, uttering sounds that denoted dissatisfaction with matters somewhere. I was busy, and at first paid no attention to her; but she grew more persistent, so that I finally laid down my letters and asked: "What is it, Puss? Haven't you had breakfast enough?" I went out to the kitchen, and she followed, all the time protesting articulately. She would not touch the meat I offered, but evidently wanted something entirely different. Just then my sister came down and said:--

"I wish you would go up and see H. She is suffering terribly, and I don't know what to do for her."

At that the Pretty Lady led the way into the hall and up the stairs, pausing at every third step to make sure I was following, and leading me straight to my sister. Then she settled herself calmly on the foot-board and closed her eyes, as though the whole affair was no concern of hers. Afterward, my sister said that when the pain became almost unendurable, so that she tossed about and groaned, the Pretty Lady came close to her face and talked to her, just as she did to her kittens when they were in distress, showing plainly that she sympathized with and would help her. When she found it impossible to do this, she hurried down to me. And then having got me actually up to my sister's bedside, she threw off her own burden of anxiety and settled into her usual calm content.

"My Goliath is at the helm now," she expressed by her attitude, "and the world is sure to go right a little longer while I take a nap."

The Codes Of Hammurabi And Moses
W. W. Davies

QTY

The discovery of the Hammurabi Code is one of the greatest achievements of archaeology, and is of paramount interest, not only to the student of the Bible, but also to all those interested in ancient history...

Religion   **ISBN:** *1-59462-338-4*   **Pages:132**
MSRP $12.95

The Theory of Moral Sentiments
Adam Smith

QTY

This work from 1749. contains original theories of conscience amd moral judgment and it is the foundation for systemof morals.

Philosophy **ISBN:** *1-59462-777-0*   **Pages:536**
MSRP $19.95

Jessica's First Prayer
Hesba Stretton

QTY

In a screened and secluded corner of one of the many railway-bridges which span the streets of London there could be seen a few years ago, from five o'clock every morning until half past eight, a tidily set-out coffee-stall, consisting of a trestle and board, upon which stood two large tin cans, with a small fire of charcoal burning under each so as to keep the coffee boiling during the early hours of the morning when the work-people were thronging into the city on their way to their daily toil...

Childrens   **ISBN:** *1-59462-373-2*   **Pages:84**
MSRP $9.95

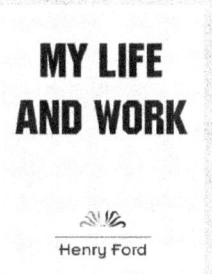

My Life and Work
Henry Ford

QTY

Henry Ford revolutionized the world with his implementation of mass production for the Model T automobile. Gain valuable business insight into his life and work with his own auto-biography... "We have only started on our development of our country we have not as yet, with all our talk of wonderful progress, done more than scratch the surface. The progress has been wonderful enough but..."

Biographies/   **ISBN:** *1-59462-198-5*   **Pages:300**
MSRP $21.95

The Art of Cross-Examination
Francis Wellman

QTY

I presume it is the experience of every author, after his first book is published upon an important subject, to be almost overwhelmed with a wealth of ideas and illustrations which could readily have been included in his book, and which to his own mind, at least, seem to make a second edition inevitable. Such certainly was the case with me; and when the first edition had reached its sixth impression in five months, I rejoiced to learn that it seemed to my publishers that the book had met with a sufficiently favorable reception to justify a second and considerably enlarged edition. ..

Pages:412

Reference   **ISBN: *1-59462-647-2***   *MSRP $19.95*

On the Duty of Civil Disobedience
Henry David Thoreau

QTY

Thoreau wrote his famous essay, On the Duty of Civil Disobedience, as a protest against an unjust but popular war and the immoral but popular institution of slave-owning. He did more than write—he declined to pay his taxes,   and was hauled off to gaol in consequence. Who can say how much this refusal of his hastened the end of the war and of slavery ?

Law   **ISBN: *1-59462-747-9***   **Pages:48**

MSRP $7.45

Dream Psychology Psychoanalysis for Beginners
Sigmund Freud

QTY

Sigmund Freud, born Sigismund Schlomo Freud (May 6, 1856 - September 23, 1939), was a Jewish-Austrian neurologist and psychiatrist who co-founded the psychoanalytic school of psychology. Freud is best known for his theories of the unconscious mind, especially involving the mechanism of repression; his redefinition of sexual desire as mobile and directed towards a wide variety of objects; and his therapeutic techniques, especially his understanding of transference in the therapeutic relationship and the presumed value of dreams as sources of insight into unconscious desires.

Pages:196

Psychology   **ISBN: *1-59462-905-6***   *MSRP $15.45*

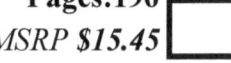
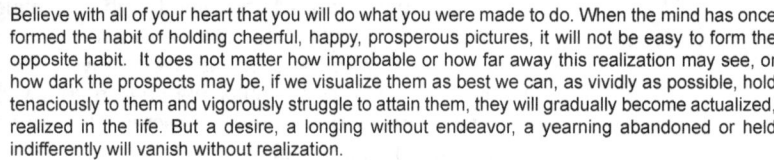

The Miracle of Right Thought
Orison Swett Marden

QTY

Believe with all of your heart that you will do what you were made to do. When the mind has once formed the habit of holding cheerful, happy, prosperous pictures, it will not be easy to form the opposite habit. It does not matter how improbable or how far away this realization may see, or how dark the prospects may be, if we visualize them as best we can, as vividly as possible, hold tenaciously to them and vigorously struggle to attain them, they will gradually become actualized, realized in the life. But a desire, a longing without endeavor, a yearning abandoned or held indifferently will vanish without realization.

Pages:360

Self Help   **ISBN: *1-59462-644-8***   *MSRP $25.45*

☐	**The Rosicrucian Cosmo-Conception Mystic Christianity** *by Max Heindel*	ISBN: *1-59462-188-8* **$38.95**

The Rosicrucian Cosmo-conception is not dogmatic, neither does it appeal to any other authority than the reason of the student. It is: not controversial, but is: sent forth in the, hope that it may help to clear... — New Age/Religion Pages 646

☐ **Abandonment To Divine Providence** *by Jean-Pierre de Caussade* ISBN: *1-59462-228-0* **$25.95**

"The Rev. Jean Pierre de Caussade was one of the most remarkable spiritual writers of the Society of Jesus in France in the 18th Century. His death took place at Toulouse in 1751. His works have gone through many editions and have been republished... — Inspirational/Religion Pages 400

☐ **Mental Chemistry** *by Charles Haanel* ISBN: *1-59462-192-6* **$23.95**

Mental Chemistry allows the change of material conditions by combining and appropriately utilizing the power of the mind. Much like applied chemistry creates something new and unique out of careful combinations of chemicals the mastery of mental chemistry... — New Age Pages 354

☐ **The Letters of Robert Browning and Elizabeth Barret Barrett 1845-1846 vol II** ISBN: *1-59462-193-4* **$35.95**

by Robert Browning and Elizabeth Barrett — Biographies Pages 596

☐ **Gleanings In Genesis (volume I)** *by Arthur W. Pink* ISBN: *1-59462-130-6* **$27.45**

Appropriately has Genesis been termed "the seed plot of the Bible" for in it we have, in germ form, almost all of the great doctrines which are afterwards fully developed in the books of Scripture which follow... — Religion/Inspirational Pages 420

☐ **The Master Key** *by L. W. de Laurence* ISBN: *1-59462-001-6* **$30.95**

In no branch of human knowledge has there been a more lively increase of the spirit of research during the past few years than in the study of Psychology, Concentration and Mental Discipline. The requests for authentic lessons in Thought Control, Mental Discipline and... — New Age/Business Pages 422

☐ **The Lesser Key Of Solomon Goetia** *by L. W. de Laurence* ISBN: *1-59462-092-X* **$9.95**

This translation of the first book of the "Lernegton" which is now for the first time made accessible to students of Talismanic Magic was done, after careful collation and edition, from numerous Ancient Manuscripts in Hebrew, Latin, and French... — New Age/Occult Pages 92

☐ **Rubaiyat Of Omar Khayyam** *by Edward Fitzgerald* ISBN:*1-59462-332-5* **$13.95**

Edward Fitzgerald, whom the world has already learned, in spite of his own efforts to remain within the shadow of anonymity, to look upon as one of the rarest poets of the century, was born at Bredfield, in Suffolk, on the 31st of March, 1809. He was the third son of John Purcell... — Music Pages 172

☐ **Ancient Law** *by Henry Maine* ISBN: *1-59462-128-4* **$29.95**

The chief object of the following pages is to indicate some of the earliest ideas of mankind, as they are reflected in Ancient Law, and to point out the relation of those ideas to modern thought. — Religiom/History Pages 452

☐ **Far-Away Stories** *by William J. Locke* ISBN: *1-59462-129-2* **$19.45**

"Good wine needs no bush, but a collection of mixed vintages does. And this book is just such a collection. Some of the stories I do not want to remain buried for ever in the museum files of dead magazine-numbers an author's not unpardonable vanity..." — Fiction Pages 272

☐ **Life of David Crockett** *by David Crockett* ISBN: *1-59462-250-7* **$27.45**

"Colonel David Crockett was one of the most remarkable men of the times in which he lived. Born in humble life, but gifted with a strong will, an indomitable courage, and unremitting perseverance... — Biographies/New Age Pages 424

☐ **Lip-Reading** *by Edward Nitchie* ISBN: *1-59462-206-X* **$25.95**

Edward B. Nitchie, founder of the New York School for the Hard of Hearing, now the Nitchie School of Lip-Reading, Inc, wrote "LIP-READING Principles and Practice". The development and perfecting of this meritorious work on lip-reading was an undertaking... — How-to Pages 400

☐ **A Handbook of Suggestive Therapeutics, Applied Hypnotism, Psychic Science** ISBN: *1-59462-214-0* **$24.95**

by Henry Munro — Health/New Age/Health/Self-help Pages 376

☐ **A Doll's House: and Two Other Plays** *by Henrik Ibsen* ISBN: *1-59462-112-8* **$19.95**

Henrik Ibsen created this classic when in revolutionary 1848 Rome. Introducing some striking concepts in playwriting for the realist genre, this play has been studied the world over. — Fiction/Classics/Plays 308

☐ **The Light of Asia** *by sir Edwin Arnold* ISBN: *1-59462-204-3* **$13.95**

In this poetic masterpiece, Edwin Arnold describes the life and teachings of Buddha. The man who was to become known as Buddha to the world was born as Prince Gautama of India but he rejected the worldly riches and abandoned the reigns of power when... — Religion/History/Biographies Pages 170

☐ **The Complete Works of Guy de Maupassant** *by Guy de Maupassant* ISBN: *1-59462-157-8* **$16.95**

"For days and days, nights and nights, I had dreamed of that first kiss which was to consecrate our engagement, and I knew not on what spot I should put my lips..." — Fiction/Classics Pages 240

☐ **The Art of Cross-Examination** *by Francis L. Wellman* ISBN: *1-59462-309-0* **$26.95**

Written by a renowned trial lawyer, Wellman imparts his experience and uses case studies to explain how to use psychology to extract desired information through questioning. — How-to/Science/Reference Pages 408

☐ **Answered or Unanswered?** *by Louisa Vaughan* ISBN: *1-59462-248-5* **$10.95**

Miracles of Faith in China — Religion Pages 112

☐ **The Edinburgh Lectures on Mental Science (1909)** *by Thomas* ISBN: *1-59462-008-3* **$11.95**

This book contains the substance of a course of lectures recently given by the writer in the Queen Street Hall, Edinburgh. Its purpose is to indicate the Natural Principles governing the relation between Mental Action and Material Conditions... — New Age/Psychology Pages 148

☐ **Ayesha** *by H. Rider Haggard* ISBN: *1-59462-301-5* **$24.95**

Verily and indeed it is the unexpected that happens! Probably if there was one person upon the earth from whom the Editor of this, and of a certain previous history, did not expect to hear again... — Classics Pages 380

☐ **Ayala's Angel** *by Anthony Trollope* ISBN: *1-59462-352-X* **$29.95**

The two girls were both pretty, but Lucy who was twenty-one who supposed to be simple and comparatively unattractive, whereas Ayala was credited, as her Bombwhat romantic name might show, with poetic charm and a taste for romance. Ayala when her father died was nineteen... — Fiction Pages 484

☐ **The American Commonwealth** *by James Bryce* ISBN: *1-59462-286-8* **$34.45**

An interpretation of American democratic political theory. It examines political mechanics and society from the perspective of Scotsman James Bryce — Politics Pages 572

☐ **Stories of the Pilgrims** *by Margaret P. Pumphrey* ISBN: *1-59462-116-0* **$17.95**

This book explores pilgrims religious oppression in England as well as their escape to Holland and eventual crossing to America on the Mayflower, and their early days in New England... — History Pages 268

www.bookjungle.com *email: sales@bookjungle.com fax: 630-214-0564 mail: Book Jungle PO Box 2226 Champaign, IL 61825*

QTY

The Fasting Cure *by Sinclair Upton*
ISBN: *1-59462-222-1* **$13.95**

In the Cosmopolitan Magazine for May, 1910, and in the Contemporary Review (London) for April, 1910, I published an article dealing with my experiences in fasting. I have written a great many magazine articles, but never one which attracted so much attention... New Age/Self Help/Health Pages 164

Hebrew Astrology *by Sepharial*
ISBN: *1-59462-308-2* **$13.45**

In these days of advanced thinking it is a matter of common observation that we have left many of the old landmarks behind and that we are now pressing forward to greater heights and to a wider horizon than that which represented the mind-content of our progenitors... Astrology Pages 144

Thought Vibration or The Law of Attraction in the Thought World
ISBN: *1-59462-127-6* **$12.95**

by William Walker Atkinson
Psychology/Religion Pages 144

Optimism *by Helen Keller*
ISBN: *1-59462-108-X* **$15.95**

Helen Keller was blind, deaf, and mute since 19 months old, yet famously learned how to overcome these handicaps, communicate with the world, and spread her lectures promoting optimism. An inspiring read for everyone... Biographies/Inspirational Pages 84

Sara Crewe *by Frances Burnett*
ISBN: *1-59462-360-0* **$9.45**

In the first place, Miss Minchin lived in London. Her home was a large, dull, tall one, in a large, dull square, where all the houses were alike, and all the sparrows were alike, and where all the door-knockers made the same heavy sound... Childrens/Classic Pages 88

The Autobiography of Benjamin Franklin *by Benjamin Franklin*
ISBN: *1-59462-135-7* **$24.95**

The Autobiography of Benjamin Franklin has probably been more extensively read than any other American historical work, and no other book of its kind has had such ups and downs of fortune. Franklin lived for many years in England, where he was agent... Biographies/History Pages 332

Name	
Email	
Telephone	
Address	
City, State ZIP	

☐ **Credit Card**   ☐ **Check / Money Order**

Credit Card Number	
Expiration Date	
Signature	

Please Mail to: Book Jungle
PO Box 2226
Champaign, IL 61825
or Fax to: 630-214-0564

ORDERING INFORMATION

web: *www.bookjungle.com*
email: *sales@bookjungle.com*
fax: *630-214-0564*
mail: *Book Jungle PO Box 2226 Champaign, IL 61825*
or PayPal *to sales@bookjungle.com*

Please contact us for bulk discounts

DIRECT-ORDER TERMS

**20% Discount if You Order
Two or More Books**
Free Domestic Shipping!
Accepted: Master Card, Visa,
Discover, American Express

www.ingramcontent.com/pod-product-compliance
Lightning Source LLC
Chambersburg PA
CBHW080745250626
47162CB00010B/3030